"The make-out room."

Spinning around, Dani was startled to see Logan looming behind her. Quickly he came forward and backed her into the small storage closet, closing the door behind them. "What did you say?" she asked breathlessly.

"That's what the guys used to call this closet. We took turns sneaking our dates back here during the dances."

Dani smiled weakly. Her heart was thudding and her throat had gone dry, but she tried to put up a good front. "We girls knew what you were doing."

"Oh yeah? We thought you did. But that just made the game more fun."

Logan pressed her against the wall. "Do you remember the last time we were in this room? We had been dancing so close to each other that we were about to melt. We came in here and kissed and kissed until our lips were bruised. I couldn't get enough of you. I—"

"Stop, Logan."

"That's what you said that night. But you didn't mean it. You wanted me as much as I wanted you."

"Don't do this to me, Logan, please," Dani pleaded.

"Why not? I want you to remember, I want you to remember just how much in love we were . . ."

WHAT ARE *LOVESWEPT* ROMANCES?

They are stories of true romance and touching emotion. We believe those two very important ingredients are constants in our highly sensual and very believable stories in the *LOVESWEPT* line. Our goal is to give you, the reader, stories of consistently high quality that may sometimes make you laugh, sometimes make you cry, but are always fresh and creative and contain many delightful surprises within their pages.

Most romance fans read an enormous number of books. Those they truly love, they keep. Others may be traded with friends and soon forgotten. We hope that each *LOVESWEPT* romance will be a treasure—a "keeper." We will always try to publish

LOVE STORIES YOU'LL NEVER FORGET
BY AUTHORS YOU'LL ALWAYS REMEMBER

The Editors

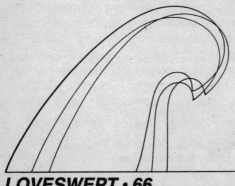

LOVESWEPT · 66

Sandra Brown
In A Class By Itself

BANTAM BOOKS
TORONTO · NEW YORK · LONDON · SYDNEY · AUCKLAND

IN A CLASS BY ITSELF
A Bantam Book / October 1984

*LOVESWEPT and the wave device are trademarks of
Bantam Books, Inc.*

ISBN 0-553-21672-4

Published simultaneously in the United States and Canada

*Bantam Books are published by Bantam Books, Inc. Its
trademark, consisting of the words ''Bantam Books'' and the
portrayal of a rooster, is Registered in U.S. Patent and Trademark Office and in other countries. Marca Registrada. Bantam
Books, Inc., 666 Fifth Avenue, New York, New York 10103.*

PRINTED IN THE UNITED STATES OF AMERICA

O   0 9 8 7 6 5 4 3 2 1

One

She was nervous.

"You're being ridiculous," she muttered to herself. "Stop it." Unfortunately, knowing such nervousness was ridiculous didn't make it miraculously disappear. And when one began talking to one's self, things had come to a sad pass.

Her clammy hands shook as she locked the car door behind her and tucked the eelskin purse under her arm. She ran one of those damp, trembling hands over her golden hair. It had been wound into a chic, tight chignon at the nape of her neck. If only her anxiety could be as easily controlled as her hair.

Taking one last deep breath, she followed the sidewalk to the Elks Lodge. Music popular a decade ago was blaring from the building. She went through the door which had been propped open to prevent a bottleneck. The bass percussion of the music hit her like a soft blow to the chest. Brilliant beams of light struck her eyes as the spotlighted mirrored ball rotated overhead. Laughter and noisy conversation rippled over her in palpable waves. Her senses were stimulated by the very vibrancy of the party, yet she stood uncertainly just inside the door.

"Dani! Oh, my heavens, it's Dani! Dani Quinn!"

The woman sitting behind the table that served as a registration desk jumped from her post and rounded the table with her arms spread wide. Dani was enclosed in a vigorous hug against breasts that were even more pillowy than they had been ten years ago. At that time those breasts had been the envy of every girl in the class; indeed, in the school.

The bearer of the enviable bosom pushed Dani back and gave her a long, thorough once-over. Disgust registered on her animated face. "I swear to God, I hate you. You haven't gained one damn pound in ten years! You're gorgeous. Gorgeous!"

Dani laughed. "Hello, Spud . . . I mean Rebecca."

"Hell, it's still Spud!" the woman shouted on a raucous laugh.

"You mean you still like french fries?"

Spud patted hips that had finally caught up to the proportions of her chest, possibly even exceeded them. "Can't you tell?"

The women laughed and hugged each other again. "You'll never change, Spud. It's so good to see you."

"And you, though we see you in the Dallas papers all the time. I was hoping that up close I would be able to see signs of age or at least detect telltale scars." She inspected Dani's hairline closely. "No face-lift. Just naturally beautiful and ageless, dammit. Stay away from Jerry," she growled.

"You and Jerry are still together?"

"Hell, yes. Who else would put up with me?"

Jerry and Spud had gone together since their sophomore year in high school. Dani envied them their uncomplicated life together. "Children?"

"Four. Heathens all. But they're with a sitter tonight and I've forgotten them for several blessed hours in which I plan to get downright tipsy." She turned back to the table. "Here's your name tag, not that anyone will have forgotten you. Most beautiful girl in the class."

"Thank you."

Spud yanked the back off the sticky side of the name tag and maternally attached it to Dani's raw silk sheath. "You put us hicks to shame, Dani. Just look at this dress." She ran her friendly gaze over Dani's svelte figure, took in the wide, braided belt with its overlarge brass buckle, the eelskin pumps that matched her handbag. "Neiman-Marcus? But then you always did make the rest of us look like we should go home and start over."

"Should I have worn jeans?"

Spud patted her arm. "Honey, class has nothing to do with clothes. You'd look just as good in a toesack." She lowered her voice and leaned closer. "Have you seen him yet?"

Dani wet her lips and averted her eyes. "Who?"

"Ah, hell, Dani. You know who. Logan."

There. It was over. Now she didn't have to dread it anymore.

For weeks, ever since she had received the photocopied letter from Spud informing her of the ten-year class reunion, she had dreaded hearing his name spoken for the first time. Well, she had survived. Her vital organs played musical chairs before they found their way back to their proper places, but she was still standing, still breathing. Admittedly, she was breathing erratically, but she *was* still breathing.

"Logan? No, I haven't seen him since . . . Well, let's see . . . it's been ten years. Is he coming?"

"Our class president? Varsity star? Of course he's coming. He's into everything that goes on in Hardwick. A regular pillar of the community. He helped me notify everyone about the reunion."

Dani's trembling hand found its way to the hammered gold medallion suspended around her neck from a strand of chunky malachite stones. "How is he?" She didn't think her air of indifference fooled Spud.

"Do you mean how does he look?" Spud laughed lustily. "Let's put it this way. I've warned Jerry that there are three men in the world I'd risk ten happy years of marriage for one night with. Robert Redford and Richard Gere are two of them."

"Oh."

"Unfortunately, Logan's always considered me his good buddy." Spud grasped Dani's arm and pushed her toward the throng. "What am I holding you here for? Go! Mix, mingle, get something to drink. A lot of people want to see you. We'll catch up on all the rest later."

Shyly at first, then, as she recognized more of her former classmates, with more enthusiasm, Dani got caught up in the party. She renewed acquaintances, met spouses, listened to capsuled versions of the last ten years. The class Romeo, who had always been on the make and after three unsuccessful marriages and six children was still on the make, took Dani under his wing.

"Dani, baby, are you thirsty? Name your poison."

"Coke, please."

His eyes widened in delighted surprise. "Our Dani has finally shed her scruples! I've heard that Greenville Avenue area of Dallas really knows how to swing. Care to teach your old buddies some new tricks?"

"Coke as in Coca-Cola, Al. On the rocks, please."

"Oh," he said, crestfallen. "Well, sure, wait right here."

Laughing to herself, she glanced down at the ballot someone had shoved into her hand. Later in the evening, when everyone had had a chance to see everyone else, they were going to award white elephant prizes for the baldest, the most changed, the one who had fathered or mothered the most children, the one who had come the farthest for the reunion, and other such categories.

"Who gets your vote?"

It had been ten years, yet she knew his voice immediately. It was deeper, more mellow. But since he was two years older than the rest of the class, by the time they'd graduated, his voice had already matured to that low timbre. It was achingly familiar and straight out of her dreams.

She raised her head and looked at him. Everything inside her stilled.

He was more handsome, more magnetic, than she remembered. With no more power than a leaf in a whirlpool, she was swept into that magic aura that surrounded him, that made him appealing to men and women alike.

Straight off a Scandinavian travel poster, his face had borne the last ten years well. Indeed, the lines faintly etched around his eyes and along either side of his mouth only added another dimension to his attractiveness.

Wheat-colored hair, as tousled as ever and defying control, fell across a wide forehead. Thick eyebrows only one shade darker than his hair sheltered eyes as crystal blue as a Texas summer sky. His slender nose flared slightly over a mouth that testified to both sensitivity and strength. The vertical cleft in his chin was deeper than she remembered, but the jaw was just as square and just as determined.

"So," he said, "who gets your vote?"

Her belly felt warm, her senses inebriated as if she had just swallowed a gulp of the strongest brandy. A steamy fog seemed to invade her peripheral vision so that everything around her faded and blurred. Only Logan's image was startlingly clear. "My vote? For which category?"

"Most Surprised To See You Here." He wasn't smiling. His eyes were busy exploring every feature of her face.

"You didn't think I'd come?"

"I didn't know."

"Why didn't you think I would?"

"I didn't think you'd have the guts."

Now he smiled. And the lazy grin was a taunting slap in the face after what he had said. Dani was affronted and hurt. Before she could reply, Al was pushing a glass of cola into her hand with such an abundance of exuberance that it sloshed over. "Oops, sorry, Dani. Hiya, Logan."

"A napkin?" Dani asked, waving the dripping cola off her hand.

"Napkin?" Al repeated stupidly. "Uh, no."

Logan somehow managed to wiggle his hand into the hip pocket of his jeans and pull out a snowy handkerchief. Unfolding it, he ceremoniously handed it to Dani. "Thank you," she said stiffly, wishing she had the courage to fling it in his face. After she had blotted her hand, she handed it back to him.

"You're welcome." His eyes stayed on her as he asked, "Which wife did you bring tonight, Al?"

"Very funny, Logan." Dismally Al sipped his Scotch. His flushed face indicated it wasn't his first. "God, man, they're bleeding me dry. I'm paying alimony and child support out the nose. Kids are always needing braces on their teeth or dance classes or God knows what."

Logan's sympathy was transparently insincere. "That's what you get for trying to populate east Texas."

"Yeah, well, you had the right idea. Love 'em and leave—Oh, damn, I'm sorry, Dani."

She wished at that moment she were anywhere on earth but there. Why had she come? It was going to be worse than she thought. "It's all right, Al." Her smile was brittle and she thought her face might crack under the pressure.

"Well," Al went on single-mindedly, "you had the right idea staying single. Marriage is a pain in the butt."

"Marriage or divorce?" Logan asked.

"In my case, they're one and the same." Even

Dani joined Logan's laughter at Al's bleak expression.

"Honey, I'm parched." A redhead sidled up to Logan and wrapped one sinuous arm around his waist. She put her other hand kittenishly on his chest.

Dani was instantly offended. The woman had a mass of red curls that surrounded her petulant face and cascaded over her shoulders. Her white satin jumpsuit was out of place for this kind of party. Its halter top barely contained her voluptuous breasts. Her nipples were rosily, grossly, apparent through the shiny cloth, a fact she seemed to take delight in as she looked up at the men through her lashes. She exuded sexual invitations with as much subtlety as a whistle blast from a rolling freight train. Dani wondered how Al's optic muscles were keeping his straining eyeballs in their sockets.

Logan draped a proprietary arm around the redhead's bare shoulders. "Lana, meet Dani Quinn. You know Al."

"Hi," she said sulkily, then turned the wide, blinking eyes toward her date. "Honey, I'm dying for something to drink."

"Okay." Turning her away, Logan said over his shoulder, "Catch you later." They headed toward the bar.

"Hell. Webster always did have all the luck with women," Al grumbled.

Dani watched the couple disappear into the crowd. Her gaze was riveted to Logan's back. He was masculinity epitomized. Broad shoulders stretched the starched cotton of his western-cut shirt. His torso tapered to a narrow waist. As she watched, Lana's restless hand slid down the groove of his spine and dipped beneath his belt at the small of his back. Dani couldn't reproach the girl. She ached to touch that shallow hollow herself.

Logan had "the walk," that saddle tramp saunter that was inherent to native Texan men, passed down through generations of cowboys. It was, without even trying to be, sexy. The unconscious roll of the hips, the slow strut, the flexed knees, the slouching stance, the deceptive laziness that hid a latent aggressiveness, were all intensely sexual. The jeans that one who had "the walk" invariably wore were always tight, snugly fitting both the front and back of his anatomy in a sex-declaring manner. Logan's jeans fit better than most. They had more to fit. They molded to his taut buttocks and long, lean thighs with breath-stopping appeal.

"That's why I never could figure it out."

Dani was brought out of her trance by Al's perplexity. "Figure what out?"

"How he ever let you get away."

She felt like gnawing her bottom lip until it bled. Instead, she said brightly, "It just wasn't meant to be."

"So," Al said, glancing around, "wanna dance with me, Dani?"

Because he was twenty-eight and looked twenty years older, because he was pitiful, and because she knew the only way she was going to survive the weekend was to brazen it out, she smiled up at him radiantly. "Sure. Why not?"

The principal of Hardwick High School, who had been there ten years ago when this class had graduated, was at the microphone. "You're fortunate tonight—" He stepped back quickly when feedback made the sound system screech loudly. He tentatively approached the mike again, dousing everyone's hope that he was finally finished. "You're fortunate tonight to have your class favorites, Logan Webster and Dani Quinn, here. As I close my little speech, I'm going to ask them to come forward and lead off the next dance. You were a class that the faculty could take pride in. Have a good time and know that you're always welcome at Hardwick High School."

There was a polite smattering of applause over the clinking of cocktail glasses and the murmur of conversation. Half the people in the room were watching Logan; the other half were watching Dani. Everyone waited expectantly.

There had been hilarity over the awards given out. Too much booze had been consumed. Diets had been blown at the buffet table. Old gossip had been spread. New gossip had been started. Everyone was enjoying himself.

But this was the evening's first moment of drama. Everyone could remember when Logan and Dani had danced exclusively with each other at every party.

Dani wished she could vaporize and not have to endure the two minutes playing time of the record that was now being placed on the turntable. She looked across the dance floor at Logan, who still had one arm casually draped over his date. Hooked between the index and middle fingers of his other hand was a long-necked bottle of beer. Palm up, he brought it to his mouth, tipped it, and took a sip, then, his eyes blazing at Dani, passed the bottle to a pouting Lana.

With the slow measured gait of a predatory animal about to devour his dinner, he came across the dance floor to stand within inches of her. "Dance, Dani?"

"I guess I have no choice."

"That's right. You have no choice. Everyone's watching. You couldn't chicken out even if you wanted to."

It was a dare, a sneaky, understated dare she couldn't refuse. Her chin went up a notch and resolution brought sparking lights to her golden eyes. Logan watched the transformation and a satisfied smile curled the corner of his lip upward. He opened his arms and she stepped into them. The crowd applauded.

"Yea, Dani! Yea, Logan!" Dani heard Spud's loud cheerleader voice cry out.

They were subjected to hoots, hollers, and wolf whistles as Logan drew her closer, his enclosing arms firmly securing her against him. He held her in the old way, with both arms tightly linked around her waist. There was nothing for her arms to do but to rest on his shoulders.

"Lana's watching."

"Who gives a damn?"

"She will. You're holding me too close."

"It's a slow dance."

She could feel his breath in her hair. She could feel everything. As though they had been asleep for years, her senses now awakened with an intense craving to experience everything they had missed. She was feeling deliciously reckless and knew that her gaze was provocative when she lifted her eyes to his. "Did you want it to be a slow dance?"

"Yes."

"Why?"

"Dumb question, Dani." He couldn't move any closer because they were already touching everywhere. But he pressed into her. "So I could hold you. See if you've changed."

"You would remember?"

"I would remember."

"And?"

"There've been some changes here and there."

"Where and where?" She smiled coquettishly.

"Here and there." As he spoke the words, his gaze sliced from one of her breasts to the other.

Self-consciousness deflated her smile. "Oh."

A rumbling chuckle hummed through his wide chest into hers. "Embarrassed?"

"You never talked to me like that before."

"Ah, but I was a callow youth with sweaty palms then. I'm a man now and can say exactly what's on my mind." He squeezed her playfully. "I'm impressed with your mature figure."

"I'll never catch up with Spud."

He laughed. "Poor Jerry. He'll go through life knowing that just about every guy in the class tried his damnedest to cop a feel of his wife."

"Did you?"

"What?"

" 'Cop a feel.' "

"I think I tried when we were in the eighth grade. She clouted me on the side of the head. I saw stars for a week and never had the courage to try again."

Other couples had joined them on the crowded dance floor so they were no longer so conspicuous.

They smiled at each other, but Logan's smile faded as he gazed at her with hot eyes. "You look good, Dani."

"Thank you."

"Don't say that," he hissed angrily. "I'm not passing out idle compliments. You know you're as beautiful as you ever were. More beautiful. And you know that your particular brand of beauty appeals to me mightily." As if to show her just how much, his arms tightened another degree. Their thighs aligned, bellies pressed together, hips meshed. Her breasts were flattened against his hard chest.

The music stopped.

She tried to move from his embrace, but he wouldn't allow it. "Logan, the music," she said breathlessly, avoiding his gaze for fear it would scorch her.

"It'll start again."

"But your date," she reminded him feebly as the strains of another slow ballad filled the room.

"She'll wait."

"You're confident of that?"

"No. It's just that I don't give a damn if she doesn't."

"That's not a very flattering thing to say."

He scoffed. "If Lana thinks there's a good time in it, she can be rented for the night."

"That's the kind of relationship you have with women now?"

"Sure. Nice and uncomplicated. What have I got to lose?"

"Self-respect."

He laughed harshly, but there was no humor in the eyes that glared down into hers. "I lost my self-respect a long time ago, Dani. When you—"

"Please, Logan, don't."

It was the way she said his name that dissolved his anger. That, coupled with how she bent her head forward and rested her forehead on his chest. It completely undid him. Anger gave way to a compulsion to hold her tight, to take her for his, to protect and love her as he had always wanted to.

He held her just as securely, but there was a gentleness to his embrace now. He looked down at the crown of her head and longed to plant a soft kiss in the part of her hair. Her hair was still pale and lustrous, moonlight and honey spun together.

Her body was dainty and compact, yet utterly feminine. As they slowly swayed to the music, he could hear the soft rustle of her clothes against his. He yearned to peel them away layer by layer, to see the texture and color of her skin, to compare it with his.

Her fragrance had the sweet, spicy headiness of plumeria and the light elusiveness of citrus flowers. He longed to nuzzle her ear with his nose, to touch the diamond stud in her earlobe with his lips, to feel the peach-fuzziness against his tongue. He wanted to taste her. All of her.

He brought one of his hands up and lowered hers from around his neck. Their hands clasped tightly. Dani's fingers relaxed and uncurled, stretched between his, and slid down into his palm to examine the calluses there.

"I still work hard for my living, Dani."

"On that farm your folks had?"

"Not exactly. Same land, but . . . Well, you'll see it tomorrow. That's where the picnic is. At my place."

"Do your parents live there with you?"

He shook his head. "They moved into town. They're both old now and keep a small house."

"I know you've made a success of your life. I read about you in *Texas Monthly*."

"A real rags to riches story, isn't it?"

"I never doubted you could do it."

"But others did. Like your parents," he added bitterly.

Her gaze fell away and that angered him. "Tell me, Dani, what would they think if they saw us dancing together now? Would these dirt farmer hands still be too dirty to touch you?"

"That was a long time ago, Logan."

"Not so long ago that I've forgotten. Am I clean enough, good enough, rich enough, to touch you now, Dani?"

"It never mattered to me!" she cried softly.

"Oh, but it did," he said silkily, leaning over her. "When it came to the showdown, it mattered a helluva lot!"

"Let me go." She pushed against his chest and forced him to release her. Turning blindly, she bumped into Al.

"Ready for another partner, Dani?" he asked drunkenly.

"Not now, Al. I'm going to the ladies' room."

She fled from the dance floor and found the rest room where she remembered it to be. She and the other girls had clustered there to share combs and lipstick and gossip during every dance Dani could remember. Now she sought the privacy of one of the stalls, not wanting to face anyone until she had composed herself.

Logan had held her and it had been blessedly, painfully, the same. But not quite the same. They were no longer children blissfully in love. Both of them had lost their innocence through heartache. She was no longer a girl finding romance in everything, thinking that the end of the story would be as marvelous as the final pages of a fairy tale.

She was a woman now. Her desires had matured and refined. Where once she had been naive about her need for Logan, where once the urgings of her body had been a mystery, an unknown quantity, she now knew exactly what she wanted. All of him. Full and hard and deep inside her.

But her predicament was the same. She couldn't have him. It was more impossible now than it had been then.

Calming herself, she left the rest room and went through the deserted hallway toward the dance hall. On her left, she passed a door and on impulse opened it. It was a storage closet, just as cozy as she remembered it.

"The make-out room."

Spinning around, she was startled to see Logan looming behind her. He came forward imperiously and backed her into the small space, closing the door behind them. "What did you say?" she asked breathlessly.

"That's what the guys used to call it. The make-out room. We took turns tricking our dates into coming back here during the dances. I wonder if the Elks know just how legendary their storage closet is?"

She smiled weakly. Her heart was thudding and her throat had gone dry, but she tried to put up a good front. "We girls knew what you were doing."

"Oh yeah? We thought you did. But that just

made the game more fun." He took another step forward. The wall behind her blocked any retreat.

She didn't want him to know how helplessly trapped she felt. "It's been wonderful seeing you again, Logan. I was just on my way out and—"

"Do you remember the last time we were in here together?"

"What about Lana?"

"What about her?" he demanded impatiently.

"She'll be looking for you."

"No, she won't. I gave her to Al." He came nearer. "Forget Lana, forget everything except the last time we were in this room. Do you remember?"

"No. I mean, yes. I'm not sure. I'm leaving now, Logan. Good night."

He grabbed her arm as she tried to squeeze past him, and pressed her against the wall. "You remember. And so do I. You had on a pink dress. It was off one shoulder and had a ruffle here." His hand cut a burning swath from one shoulder across her breasts to beneath the opposite arm. She moaned softly. Every erogenous cell in her body was sounding alarm signals. "You had tiny pearls in your ears and a single strand here." His finger traced the base of her throat and stayed to tickle and stroke. "Your hair was pulled up, but you had curls that touched your cheeks, here." He tugged gently at strands of hair around her face until they fell from the sleek hairdo to caress her cheeks.

The memory was vivid, but she denied it, both to herself and to him. "I don't remember."

"Yes, you do." His voice was as close as his body, just as compelling, just as urgent.

She turned to face the wall, giving him her back.

But he wasn't deterred. He stepped close enough for her to feel his breath on the back of her neck, to feel his thighs against the backs of hers, his hardness against her bottom.

"We had been dancing so close, rubbing against each other until we were about to melt. We came in here and kissed and kissed till our lips were bruised. You were delicious and sweet and I couldn't get enough of your mouth. When I begged you to touch me, you pulled my shirttail out of my pants and laid your hands on my chest."

"Stop, Logan."

"That's what you said then. When I touched your breasts, you said 'no.' But you didn't want me to stop. Not really. I went on touching you, petting you, until we were both on fire. You wanted me just as much as I wanted you."

"Don't do this," she pleaded raggedly. Her head dropped forward, but that only allowed him to place his lips against the back of her neck.

"Why not? I want you to remember. I want you to remember how much in love we were."

"I do."

"Do you? Then why didn't you tell your parents how we felt about each other?"

She whirled around to face him. "I did!"

"Obviously they weren't convinced," he growled. "Can you imagine how I felt when you chose them over me?"

"I had no choice."

"You were eighteen. You were legally independent. You had a choice."

"I didn't!" she shouted. For a long, silent moment the words reverberated around them.

"Well, you chose to come back now," he said with

slow precision. He inclined toward her until they were touching full length, breast to knees. "You left with them then, but you're here with me now."

The white-hot gleam in his blue eyes frightened her, but she made a vain attempt at bravado. "Let me go, Logan. We're not kids necking in the coat closet any longer."

"You're damned right we're not. I want a helluva lot more than a few minutes of necking from you." She tried to twist away from him, but his body only sealed hers more firmly to the wall. "You should never have come back, Dani. Not unless you wanted me to collect my debt."

Her throat was congested with fear and passion. "What debt? What do you want from me?"

"You've gotta be kidding. You know what I want." He lowered his face over hers until their lips were scarcely an inch apart. "You owe me a wedding night."

Two

For more than a minute she stared up at him, paralyzed, unable to move, to think, to breathe. Shock sustained her for an instant and then the import of what he had said began to sink in.

"You don't mean that," she whispered.

"I certainly do."

"Not literally."

"Most literally," he said with soft emphasis.

She licked her lips, praying he would move away. He was still pressed so close, she was intimately aquainted with each rigid plane of his body. The fly of his jeans was imprinted on her silk dress. From that point of contact heat emanated throughout her body. Her breasts ached for his touch. Caresses she'd denied remembering, she now craved.

Such desires couldn't be acknowledged. How could she make him see reason when every aspect of him told her he was deadly serious? He was a man who had been sexually thwarted. The disappointment and frustration had had ten years to fester inside him.

"Logan, we were children," she pleaded earnestly.

"We were young, yes. But not children. Children don't know what they're doing. We did, Dani. We knew exactly what we were doing. We knew what we wanted. Each other."

She groped for a comeback. It was a familiar argument, one she had been having with herself for ten years, and she always lost. How could she expect to win against him? "I'll grant you we wanted each other physically, but we didn't realize—"

"If that's all I'd wanted, Dani, I wouldn't have held off for the two years we dated." A pained, self-derisive smile twisted his mouth. "I was going with the most beautiful girl in the class, the one every guy would have given his eyeteeth for just one date with. But you were also the nicest girl, the one who didn't put out."

"Do you expect an apology?"

"No."

"I didn't realize what a tremendous sacrifice you were making," she said sarcastically.

"A sacrifice, yes. But not tremendous. I wanted to be with you on any terms."

"So why bring up my morals now?"

She had strained his temper to the breaking point. "Because I want you to understand that I didn't marry you just to get laid. I loved you, dammit."

He gripped her shoulders hard. "I wasn't thinking only of the wedding night when we ran off to find a justice of the peace. I was thinking of the rest of our lives together. I went through that ceremony with a naive reverence for what we were pledging to each other. To me, it wasn't just parroting words that would legalize going to bed with you. It meant something."

He was breathing hard and his fingers bit into the flesh of her upper arms. "Do you know how humiliating it was to step out of the justice of the peace's office a bridegroom, only to be arrested? For God's sake, Dani, put yourself in my place. Try to imagine how I felt."

She had been holding herself rigid. Now, as she remembered the flashing red and blue lights, the noise, the confusion, the anger on her parents' faces, the outrage on Logan's, she slumped against him. "I felt the same way. If you remember so well, then you remember that when they dragged you into that sheriff's car, I was screaming hysterically. I begged them not to hurt you."

"All I saw was you being consoled by your mother and father, as though I'd kidnapped you or something."

"They were justifiably worried. It was irresponsible of us to run away like that."

"Then you condone your father having me arrested for stealing your car?"

"No, no," she said miserably. "That was a ghastly thing for him to do. He didn't know any other way to stop us."

"Well, it was a damned effective way. It worked." His hands slid from her arms. "He dropped the charges, but not before I spent a few nights in jail while they hustled you off to Dallas and had the marriage annulled."

All the wretchedness of those days came rolling over her in smothering waves. She had wept, pleaded, bargained, threatened to run away, threatened suicide, if they didn't let her see Logan. Her parents had remained adamant. He wasn't for her, they said. He would make her miserably unhappy. He couldn't provide the standard of life they wanted for her, the standard she was accustomed to. He wasn't their "kind." When all her energies had been exhausted, she had lived in a daze for months.

"I went to Dallas and finally got to see your father," Logan said. "By then, you and your mother had gone to Europe. He told me you regretted what you had done and never wanted to see me again."

"I never said that," she said with the same listlessness she had felt then. "That trip was forced on me. We stayed for six months. When we got back, I could see that it was hopeless."

He took hold of her again and shook her slightly. "It wasn't hopeless. Not until you gave in. If only you had fought them harder."

"But I couldn't. They were my parents."

"And I was your *husband.*" The words were harsh and had a finality to them that made her shudder, whether out of fear or expectation, she couldn't say. "I had a bride, Dani, but never a wife. I intend to get what's coming to me."

She tried to shake free of his hold and was dimly disappointed when he let her go. "That's impossible."

He laughed softly and let his index finger drift

over her lower lip. "Far from impossible. We're both healthy, consenting adults."

She swatted his hand away. "I'm not consenting."

"You will be," he stated with an assurance that infuriated her. "I would never have come to Dallas after you, but you're on my turf now. And whatever ventures onto my territory, I claim as mine."

"That sounds like a threat."

"It is. Or a promise, depending on how you look at it."

"It's an empty threat, Logan. I'll leave and go back to Dallas tonight."

He caught the medallion around her neck and pulled her forward until her head was bent back at an unnatural angle. His lips were so close to hers, she could feel them moving before she heard his sibilantly spoken words. "And convince me once again what a coward you are? I don't think so, Dani." She could taste the kiss that never materialized, and again felt disappointed.

He released her. "See you tomorrow." He took several steps backward as he treated her to an insolent grin, then let himself out of the closet, closing the door behind him.

"Damn!"

Dani flung her purse onto the bed in her motel room and threw herself down beside it. Lying on her back, she kicked off her shoes. She stared up at the ceiling, seeing Logan's smug grin as he left her. She thumped her fists on the uncomfortable mattress. "Of all the arrogant . . . ."

But her fury lacked conviction and she knew it. Rolling to her side, she drew herself into a ball and rested her cheek on her hand. He was arrogant and self-confident and a tad conceited. He was a born leader, a shining golden god toward whom people automatically gravitated. He was fun and generous and, in most instances, kind. She knew he wanted to hurt her the way he had been hurt. But she knew equally well that he wouldn't deliberately abuse anyone.

And she knew that for all those reasons, she still loved him.

"Oh, God, what am I going to do?"

Had it been a monumental error in judgment to come back to Hardwick? Time and again she had almost talked herself out of returning for the reunion. But she had been inexorably drawn back, masochistically compelled to see what he was like, what his life was like now. The magazine article hadn't mentioned a Mrs. Webster and a family, but Dani had had no guarantee that she wouldn't find him happily married. If she had, she probably would have died from the pain of it.

But wouldn't that have been better than the predicament she found herself in now? She should leave. Tonight. But if she did, she would be letting down so many people who were counting on her.

It had all happened so innocently. She had been at a committee meeting and they were discussing plans for a fund-raising luncheon.

"I won't be in town that Friday," Dani remembered saying. "I'm going to Hardwick for my ten-year class reunion."

"Hardwick?" The chairwoman's ears had perked up like a hungry wolf's. "That's in east Texas, isn't it?"

"About three hours drive from here," Dani had

said. "It's a small town. My father used to have a timber business there."

Mrs. Meneffee had gone to her desk and rifled through a drawer until she located a map. She studied it for a minute, then excitedly exclaimed, "That's what I thought. Dani, Hardwick isn't too far from that old church camp we're trying to buy."

"Oh?"

"Yes. And the owner of all that land lives in Hardwick. I'm almost sure." She was leafing through her notebook. "Yes! Mr. Logan Webster. He's into cattle, real estate, no oil, but natural gas, I think. He bought that old camp a few years ago, but has never done anything with it. We've corresponded with him in hopes that he might sell it to us. So far we haven't heard from him."

Dani was one of the founders of Friends of Children. Its sole purpose was to raise funds for retarded and handicapped children. It had long been a dream of hers to have a summer camp for these children to enjoy.

"Do you know him?" Mrs. Meneffee asked her.

When the incisive gaze, which could intimidate a hundred dollar bill out of the tightest of fists, bore down on her, Dani averted her eyes. "Yes." She cleared her throat. "At least, I've heard of him."

"While you're over there, why don't you pay him a call? If anyone can talk him into selling the land cheaply for our cause, you can."

The woman had persisted, had overcome all of Dani's feeble arguments, and eventually had won Dani's promise to see Mr. Webster while she was in Hardwick.

"Well, I've seen him," she said flatly to her image

in the bathroom mirror as she began to undress. "And I don't think he's in a very generous mood."

He wanted to take, not give. And what he wanted to take . . .

She shivered as she slipped into a nightgown. On her way to bed, her eye happened to catch a glimpse of the briefcase lying on the table. She went to it and took out the leaflets and brochures she had brought with her.

Children stared out at her from numerous photographs and her heart turned over, as it always did. Her work was so important, more important than her personal problems. When one compared her life to the hardship these children and their families experienced every day, her anxieties seemed selfish and petty.

Switching out the light, she knew that tomorrow she would follow the map Spud had given her with directions to Logan's house.

She had made a promise to speak to Logan about the land. More important, she had made a commitment years ago. And nothing, not even Logan's threat, could keep her from fulfilling that commitment.

"I'd love to hate you, you know." Spud was munching on the corner of a tortilla chip. Dani was sitting across from her at the glass-topped patio table. The fringe on the shade umbrella ruffled in the warm summer breeze.

Dani laughed. "Why?"

"*Why?* Look at you. You don't sweat. I think she's an alien," Spud said to her husband in a stage whisper.

"Who's an alien?" Logan came up behind Spud in time to hear her comment.

"Dani. She doesn't sweat. Her hair is never messed up. And she's been swimming! Me, I swim and I come out looking like a disheveled water buffalo. She emerges from the water like some damn mermaid."

Logan bent at the knee to peer under the umbrella at Dani. As they stared at each other the sounds of cavorting swimmers, the shouts of those playing a vigorous game of volleyball, the chatter around them, dissolved into nothingness. "She looks good enough to eat," Logan said softly.

Dani blushed beneath her wide-brimmed straw hat and the tinted frames of her oversized sunglasses couldn't hide her lowered lashes. Under the halter sundress that covered her bikini, her skin glowed hot at Logan's ardent gaze.

"Could I borrow your reed-thin body for just one afternoon?" Spud asked her.

Thankful for Spud's interference, Dani asked jokingly, "And do what with it?"

"Run naked on the beach."

Logan hooted and bent down to hug Spud. Lecherously he whispered in her ear, "Why would you want another body to do that? It would be a real treat to see yours against surf and sand. I'd buy a ringside seat."

Spud's eyes opened wide. "You would? You've noticed! After all these years I find out that Logan Webster has looked at my body and lusted in his heart?"

Logan flashed her a dazzling smile. "Lots of times."

"Jerry, did you hear that? Are you insanely jealous?" Spud demanded of her husband.

"Insanely." He took a bored sip of his margarita. By now they had attracted a crowd and everyone was laughing. Jerry went on in a bland voice. "I can't hang every guy who's ogled you, Spud. They were willing to look and not touch. I married you."

"But . . . but you always said that my "—she gestured with her hands—"my, you know, had nothing to do with the way you felt about me."

Jerry's homely face split into a guilty grin. "I lied."

"Jerry Perkins! Is that why you always wanted to sit by me on the football bus?" His sappy grin was a giveaway. "Well, I never!"

"Yes, you did," Jerry reminded her with a lewd wink. "Many times."

"Ooh!" Spud puffed up. Then her good nature got the best of her and she began to laugh. "I did, didn't I? Well, what the hell, I loved every minute of it and still do. Pass the nachos."

Through the resultant laughter, one of the former class athletes said, "We never had so much fun as when the cheerleaders got to ride back from the out-of-town games in the football bus."

"Yeah, remember? Let's see, there was Jerry and Spud."

"Logan and Dani."

"For sure. How'd you always manage to beat everyone else to the back seat, Webster?"

"They were always so wrapped up in each other, they were *bo*-ring."

Logan's eyes locked with Dani's across the table.

"Remember the kissing tournament we held all the way back from Lampasas?"

"French kissing or it didn't count," Spud reminded them.

"Who won?"

"Who do you think? Logan and Dani. They went on for miles after everyone else had come up for air."

"Hell, I was only half a mile behind," Jerry said grumpily.

Everyone laughed. Everyone but two, who were still staring at each other.

"Who else was in on that contest? Oh, Janey and P.J."

"Where is Janey? I thought she'd be here."

"She lives in Beaumont. Just had a baby, her third, and couldn't come."

"P.J.'s in California, practicing law, married. Heard his wife is a lawyer too."

"No kiddin'?"

The talk went on around Dani and Logan. It didn't affect their absorption in each other.

"Remember Billy Clyde what's his name?"

"Winslow?"

"Yeah, Billy Clyde Winslow. Joined the Army. Went to Cambodia and came back bonkers. Way over the edge."

"Drugs?"

"Guess so."

Logan was looking at Dani's mouth. She could *feel* him studying it. His eyes were trained on her lips, and her lips felt full and swollen beneath his burning gaze. In turn, she studied his mouth, the cleft in his chin, and remembered those nights on the football bus. It was invariably drafty. Chilly fall winds would whistle through the rattling windows, yet she would be so warm. They would cuddle under his jacket. Their lips would cling until they were both breathless; his hands would explore, leaving her body feverish and aching.

They hated to see the city limit sign come into sight, and wished they could ride in the darkened bus to the edge of the world, wrapped in each other's arms. When he left her at her front door, she would feel languid and excited, wonderfully tired and yet exhilarated. Her heart would be pounding in time to her light and shallow breathing. Between her thighs there would be a deliciously forbidden moistness.

She suffered all those symptoms now, just looking at him.

"Logan?"

Lana's purring voice cut into Dani's thoughts like a blaring trumpet. "Al wants to rub some of that tanning oil on me. Where did I leave it last time I was here?" She had on a crocheted bikini that barely covered the essentials. A slender gold chain clung seductively to her hips, dropping a charm shaped like a pair of lips directly above her mound.

Logan looked at her as though she were an irritating child. Officially she was his date for the weekend. He wished she would just vanish. All day she had been coming on to poor Al. If she hoped to make Logan jealous, she was wasting her time. Still, he hated to be rude. "I don't know where it is, Lana. Check the cabana." When he turned back around, Dani had excused herself and was wending her way through the crowd toward the house.

She entered the spacious kitchen through one of the numerous patio doors. Taking off her hat and sunglasses, she set them aside and pressed her palms to her warm cheeks, hoping to cool them.

She gazed around the room. It was as gorgeous as the rest of the house, which had amazed her. Ten years ago, she had had a vague idea of where the Webster farm was, though Logan had never taken her there. The roads had changed since then and she thought she had surely taken the wrong turn when the map led her up a tree-lined lane to a sprawling modern ranch house.

Built of stone and cedar, it was a marvel of architecture, with wide glistening windows and intricate angles. The pool and cabana were surrounded by semitropical plants and lush flower beds. Behind the horse barn and other outbuildings, acres of rolling pastureland resembling a green lake eventually undulated into dense piney woods. She remembered Logan telling her that his family's farm encompassed a few measly acres. Apparently he had bought a vast amount of acreage surrounding the original plot, torn down the old house, and begun his own empire.

The interior was magnificent. Quarry tile floors dotted with area rugs connected all the open airy rooms. Modern but comfortable furniture, upholstered in natural fabrics, made the rooms look homey despite the vaulted ceilings. The kitchen was sunlit and modern. But now it was completely littered. The party had generated a staggering amount of refuse. Dani began putting the trash into a large plastic bag.

"*That's* bound to be a novelty for you."

Glancing over her shoulder, she saw Logan's silhouette filling the doorway. "What?"

"Doing maid service. Don't you have a maid who usually does this kind of thing for you?"

She bit her lip to keep the sharp retort inside. They hadn't been alone all day. Now that they were, he was deliberately baiting her, but she mustn't rise to it. She had a mission to accomplish, and if it killed her, she was going to get on Logan's good side.

Turning back to the sink, she began to rinse out glasses and put them into the dishwasher. "No, I don't have a maid. I live alone in a small condominium. There's not enough housework to keep *me* occupied, much less a maid."

"No maid. A small condominium. You drive a modest Buick." Coming to stand near her, he braced his bottom against the countertop, folded his arms across his chest, crossed his ankles, and leaned back to face her. The well-fitting trousers cupped his sex in a most disconcerting way. "Didn't your husband agree to alimony?"

Her head snapped up and her hands froze in midair. The glass she was holding dripped sudsy water onto the floor. She hadn't thought he'd know she'd been married. Her divorce settlement was none of his damn business and she started to point that out to him.

But his grin was purposely goading and she refused to be provoked. She lowered the glass to the dishwasher, well aware that when she bent to do so, her hip pressed against Logan's hard thigh.

"There was no alimony. I didn't want it. I wanted nothing from him. Not even his name."

"Your marriages don't last very long, do they? Did the other sucker at least get you into his bed before you bolted?"

She slammed the dishwasher closed and whirled to face him. Her hands were balled into fists at her sides, the nails biting into her palms. Through lips stiff with anger she said, "My marriage—"

"Which one?"

"The real one."

"Ours was real."

"Okay, the *second* one was a big mistake."

"I heard he had a five million dollar house in Turtle Creek, old Dallas money, memberships to the best clubs, and oil royalties that would make a sheik jealous. That sounds right up your alley, Dani."

That hurt her to the quick. Did he think no more of her than that? Her brow wrinkled and her lips parted with heartache. "Excuse me," she said softly, and turned to go.

Her wrist was loosely but inescapably grasped by long, tapering fingers, and she was brought up short. She kept her back to him as he tugged gently at her hand. "I'm sorry. That was a rotten thing to say. Why didn't you slap me?" When she still didn't turn around, his fingers crept up her arm to its sensitive biceps and encircled it warmly. "Dani. Look at me." She turned, her eyes swimming with tears. "I'm sorry."

"You're terribly unfair, Logan. You treat everyone else kindly. Why do you hurt me?"

"You should know," he said softly.

"Because I hurt you."

"Something like that."

"We can't change the past."

"I'm going to try."

His blue-eyed gaze was so hot that she had to look away from it or melt. His soft chuckle brought her head up. "Don't look so worried. I'm not going to force my husbandly rights on you. Particularly with such a large audience." He nodded toward the patio where the others seemed not to have missed them. "Come on, I know where we can talk." He dragged her outside through another set of doors so they would avoid the crowd.

"Where are we going?"

"Someplace where no one will eavesdrop. And if they do overhear, they won't repeat anything."

"Where are you taking me—the barn?"

"Or the airplane hangar."

"The barn. I'd love to see your horses."

Barn was hardly the word to use for the building he led her to. It was thoroughly modern and well maintained. Logan slid the huge door open, and before she knew his intent, he scooped her up in his arms to carry her inside.

"What are you doing?"

"You're not exactly dressed in barn attire and I wouldn't want you to step in anything unpleasant." He tilted his head toward her feet, which were shod only in a pair of sandals with slender thongs wrapped around her ankles.

"I think there's little chance of that. This place looks cleaner than most houses."

But she didn't try to win her release. They gazed at each other happily until they became aware of each other in a new way. His arm was hard against her bare back. She could feel the strength of it, could feel the crisp hairs against her skin. He knew the satiny texture of her bare legs draped over his other arm. Her own arms were looped loosely around his neck. Their faces were close.

"Aren't I heavy?" she asked huskily. Her breast

was pressed against the solid wall of his chest. It felt right and wonderful.

"You never were."

He walked down the center aisle of the barn, stopping at each stall to introduce her to the horse inside. When they were at the far end, he deposited her on a covered barrel and stepped back. "What do you think?" His pride in the animals was obvious.

"I think they're all beauties."

God, she was the beauty, he thought. Sunlight filtered through the small window and fell on her like a diffused spotlight. Her hair, still damp from her swim, had been drawn into a ponytail. It caught each sunbeam before throwing it back into his eyes. Her skin shone almost translucent. Dust motes danced around her, ecstatic in their right to be near such loveliness. She looked like she had been spawned by the sun, with her golden hair and golden eyes, a package of sunlight in the wrapping of a beautiful woman.

They smiled their pleasure at the sight of the other. But Dani noted a frown beginning in the deep furrow between his brows. "You were smiling a moment ago. Now you're frowning."

"What happened to your marriage, Dani?"

Sighing, she propped herself against the top of the barrel and swung her legs back and forth. "He was exactly what my parents wanted."

"I could have guessed that. And you?"

"I was terribly unhappy and therefore vulnerable. Ready to reach out for anything. He was charming and gay and always dashing off to one party or another. I thought maybe the diversions he provided would be an answer to my melancholia."

"They weren't?"

"No."

"Is that why you divorced him?"

"That, along with . . . many things." She said it in a way that told him the topic was closed to further discussion.

"You've lived alone since then?" He tried to sound casual, but she wasn't deceived.

"You mean, have there been any men in my life? No. Can you say the same thing about women?"

His eyes flashed fiercely, then cooled appreciably, and he looked away. "I'm a man, Dani."

"And that excuses your indiscretions? You're a man so you're allowed casual affairs and recreational sex?" When she saw his shoulders bunch in anger, she sighed. "Never mind. I know about your sexual escapades. I've been well informed by our classmates who still live in town."

"Don't believe everything you hear. Most of it is speculation."

"Based on some truth?"

"Based on some truth," he conceded grudgingly.

She studied him for a moment. "You like being who you are now, don't you, Logan?"

He pondered that for a moment before saying, "Yes, I do. I guess I should apologize for being proud of what I've done, of how far I've come, but damned if I will. None of it came easy."

He stood before her almost angrily, certainly defiantly. "You know I was two years older than everybody else in the class. Do you know why? Because when I was just a kid, I had to stay home and help out or we wouldn't have been just poor. We'd have been hungry. I missed school and the teachers kept me back two years so I could catch up. I had to be a good athlete, a good student. I had to win peer approval because we were poor. Otherwise I would have been ridiculed.

"While you were going to sorority parties at SMU, I was working my buns off trying to pay my way through Tech and sending money home too. It took me five years just to get a bachelor's degree. But I finally did, and when I came back, I was dead set on making something of myself."

"You never had to prove anything to anybody, Logan. You always were something."

He stubbornly shook his head. "But not something good enough. I wasn't good enough to have the woman I wanted." She looked down at her hands, but he placed a finger under her chin and roughly jerked her head upright again. "You know that timber business your father sold when he moved you back to Dallas? I own it now. And it's doing twice the business it did when he had it. That was why you moved here our sophomore year, wasn't it? So your father could get that new sideline of his going?"

"Yes. But that's ancient history. I'm happy for you, Logan. Not surprised, though. I knew you had the makings of a success."

"But not the makings of a providing husband for my wife."

"I didn't think that. My parents did."

"But you listened to them!" he shouted.

"Yes. At the time, yes. I was frightened, scared by what we'd done. Yes, I listened to them then."

"Ah, Dani." He moved close to her and pulled her head against his chest. His head bent low over hers. He rubbed her bare back. "How can I blame you for what you did? You didn't know how to be anything but what you were. You didn't know what it was like to be poor. It was natural for you to go to SMU and get a degree in psychology that you'll never use."

"I use it," she mumbled into his chest, but he seemed not to hear her.

"It was natural for you to behave exactly as you behaved." He lifted her head by cradling her cheeks between his palms. "Only, understand me too. I've had to scrape and save and fight for everything I've got." He dropped a quick, light kiss on her mouth. "I'm still fighting."

Then his mouth came down hard to claim hers.

Three

Oh, dear heaven, it felt good. This kiss. His mouth. Warm and firm, yet soft, it moved over hers with gentle sipping motions. His beard-rough chin left a tingling abrasion on hers. His musky cologne mingled with the warm smell of the hay. The atmosphere teemed with life, fecundity, nature in its most elemental form. And they were part of it. She felt small and defenseless against his muscular, powerful, athletic body. Her femininity blossomed in response to his sheer virility.

He settled his lips on the corner of her mouth and teased it with feathery strokes of his tongue. "God, you're sweet. Dani, Dani. It's been so long since I've tasted you."

"So long."

"Let me taste you again."

"Logan."

The sure thrust of his tongue parted her lips. His

tongue sank into the honeyed welcome of her mouth, probing deeper and deeper, stroking, exploring, savoring. Filaments of ecstasy spiraled up from the heart of her womanhood to curl beguilingly in her stomach and around her breasts, drawing them tight. Wonderful sensations fluttered inside her until she thought she could take flight.

Her hands came up and wandered aimlessly over Logan's shoulders until her fingers tunneled into the thick tawny hair on the back of his neck.

He made a low animal sound in his throat. Moving his hands from her back to her sides, he spread his fingers wide over her ribs and lifted her from the barrel. The instant her toes touched the ground, he gathered her close and conformed her body to his. The palms of his hands slid up and down her sides below her raised arms. One hand moved past her waist to open over her hips and press her into his hard heat.

Their breath staggered through their lips as they drew apart slightly. He brushed her face with light, quick, random kisses. "Tell me this feels good," he whispered roughly.

"This feels good."

He kissed her again. His mouth took hers with supple ardency. He was bold, thorough, evocative, and when he finally lifted his head, she knew it had been more than a kiss. His mouth had made love to hers.

"You never kissed me like that ten years ago," she murmured against his moist lips.

"I wouldn't have dared." His middle rotated slowly against hers and she moaned.

"Why?"

"Because then I didn't have the self-control to go this far and stop."

"And now you do?"

"I'm making no promises."

He lowered his head to kiss her again, but the dangerous vibration in his voice had sent warning flares to her brain. She turned her head so that she caught the kiss just below her ear. "We'd better get . . . ah, Logan . . . back. They'll be wonder—"

"Don't leave when everyone else does," he whispered against her neck with fervent urgency. "Stay with me awhile."

"I can't—"

"Yes, you can."

"I—"

His lips stopped her protest with a lingering kiss. "Stay with me, Dani. Just for a while. That's all I ask for now."

"I don't know. I'll think about it."

"When will you know?"

Should she? Should she begin something that couldn't be finished? No. If she had one grain of sense left, she would get into her car and return to Dallas and never think of this man again.

But his kisses and the gifted touch of his hands had robbed her of reason. She wanted to stay. Besides, she hadn't spoken to him about the camp yet.

Rationalization, Dani, she accused herself as his hands splayed hard and compelling over her naked back and hugged her to him protectively. Her face nestled in the V of his collar. Crinkly curls of golden hair tickled her lips. She rubbed her mouth against the soft mat. He smelled and tasted like summery outdoors and healthy man.

She had a valid reason to stay. She had promised to talk to him about the property her organization wanted to buy. Wasn't that justification enough?

Maybe. Maybe not. Why look for justification? She wanted to stay. It was as simple as that.

He had been nuzzling her neck, whisking his lips across every bare expanse of skin he could find. "When will you know?" he asked again.

She leaned back and looked up into his face. Her fingertip timidly traced the vertical dimple in his chin. "I'll stay . . . but only for a while."

"So, how goes it?" Spud flopped down in the patio chair next to Dani.

"How goes what?"

She was held spellbound watching Logan play volleyball in an exclusive men's game, which was much rowdier than the one the women had played in with them. He had changed into a pair of corduroy shorts and taken off his shirt. The late afternoon sun shone on his sweat-glossed, tanned skin. The red-gold light glistened in the golden dusting of his body hair, and made of his hair a shining helmet. He moved with sleek grace, all muscle and sinew, stretching and flexing in perfect coordination. The sight of him took her breath away, and she was once again grateful for her large hat and sunglasses, which could camouflage her agitation.

"How goes what," Spud mimicked as she eyed her entranced friend. Leaning over, she snapped her fingers in front of Dani's eyes. Dani blinked and turned toward her. "How go the libidos? Yours and Logan's. Are they singing in harmony again?"

Dani blushed. "I . . . we . . ."

"Never mind," Spud grumbled, swinging her feet up onto the chaise. "You never would tell even one juicy tidbit at any of our slumber parties. If I die before experiencing one of Logan's kisses, even by proxy, it'll be your fault."

Dani laughed and returned her attention to the game. Logan was looking at her. The ball whizzed past his head unseen. He was lambasted by his teammates and forcibly drawn back into the game.

"He never did get over it, you know," Spud said casually. Too casually.

Dani whipped her head around. "Over what?"

"Over what happened a few nights after graduation."

Dani paled. "You know?"

Spud patted her hand. "Don't worry. I'm the only one who knows about your elopement and what happened afterward. Well, Jerry too, but we're considered one."

"Logan told you?"

"Almost by accident. He had come home from Tech one Christmas vacation. We had him over for dinner. Quite innocently I brought out the clipping I'd saved about your wedding. Logan looked like he was going to barf up my delicious lasagna, then he got so furious, I thought he was going to smash the furniture we were buying on installment. That's when he told us, in angry spurts and with much foul language, what had happened that night."

She took Dani's hand and squeezed it. "I've known Logan Webster since grade school. I've never seen him like that before or since. He started drinking at our house and I don't think he stopped for about three days.

"After he graduated and came back to Hardwick, he worked like a Trojan. He was bent on making as much money as he could, as fast as he could. Jerry and I kinda thought it might be because of you. He was harder, ya know? Not the happy-go-lucky guy we'd always known. He was *driven*. He's still putting his kid brother and sister through college. Anyway, we never were brave enough to mention your name again. Not until we started planning the reunion. Then he nearly drove me crazy asking if I'd heard from you and wanting to know if you were coming."

Varied emotions were squeezing Dani's throat. Had his heart been broken? He didn't look like a man who would suffer long over the loss of an easy-to-come-by commodity like a woman. She watched Logan jump, arching up to slam his hand against the volleyball. He landed with the surefootedness of a mountain lion. He was familiar, but she was seeing him through new eyes.

His body had intrigued and frightened her when she was a sixteen-year-old watching him charge down the basketball court in shorts and tank top. Still intrigued, but no longer frightened of the sexual nature that made his body so vastly different from hers, she wanted to explore every inch of him, to discover each sweet spot of his flesh, to touch it, to taste it. She had never felt that way about any other man.

But how many women had there been who had felt the same desire for Logan? And how many women had he desired? She looked toward the poolside. Al and Lana had given up all pretense of decorum and were writhing together on a chaise.

"I'm sure that if he suffered, it was momentary,"

Dani said to Spud. "His reaction to my marriage was fleeting and was born of anger or maybe hurt pride, not unrequited love. How many women like Lana have soothed any bruises I might have left on his ego?"

Spud had seen Al and Lana, too, and she made a scoffing sound. "Too many to count," she said flatly. Dani swung her head around, surprised that Spud would admit it to her. Spud was smiling. "You thought I'd soften the blow, didn't you?" She folded her hands behind her head. "Nope. There have been many women *exactly* like Lana. But no one—ever—that he could get serious about. No one he would even consider marrying. He'll squire around a tramp like Lana for a month or two, then dump her. Probably just so folks won't think he's gone gay. But if you ask me, and Jerry thinks this, too, there's only been one love in Logan's life. And you're it, honey."

"Great party, Spud." Al, with Lana clinging to him like a wilted vine, had come up to where they were sitting. "Me and Lana, we're gonna split."

"Well, it's about time," Spud said ungraciously. "It was getting downright embarrassing."

Al looked chagrined; Lana looked smug. "Good to see you, Dani," he said. "Maybe I'll call you up if I come to Dallas."

"Come on, sugar," Lana cooed, tugging at his arm. "Let's go."

"Well, 'bye," Al said lamely.

"Invite me to your next wedding. Or divorce. Whatever," Spud called after them, laughing.

"What'd she mean, sugar?"

"Uh, nothing, Lana. Come on, baby, my car's right over here."

Just then Logan came jogging over, mopping his face and neck with a towel. "See ya, Al, Lana." He didn't sound like a man in the throes of pea green jealously.

Spud looked at Dani with an I-told-you-so tilt to her eyebrow.

Others began to drift away after exchanging addresses and promises to keep in touch until the next reunion. It was a sunburned, tired group that slowly trickled to the parked cars, but everyone agreed that the reunion had been a total success.

"You don't have to do that, Spud," Logan said. She was loading a tray with leftover food and serving dishes to carry back into the house.

"You volunteered your house. The least I can do is help you salvage it. I appointed myself a committee of one to organize this shindig, so I feel responsible for the damages." She glared at Jerry who was reclining on a glider, sipping the last of the frozen margaritas. "Jerry, get off your butt and help."

"I thought you were a committee of one," he teased.

"You'd better tread lightly, mister." Spud faced her husband belligerently, hands on hips. "I'm still mad as hell at you for making that crack about my boobs in front of everybody."

Jerry got off the glider and embraced her heartily, trying to steal a kiss. "Ah, hell, Spud. If you cared that much, you wouldn't have let them grow this big."

The next thing he knew he had landed on his back in the swimming pool. The other three dissolved into hysterical laughter at his stunned expression as he sputtered to the surface. "I'll get you back, Spud," he warned.

"Promise?" she taunted.

They managed to get the patio and kitchen back in order. As she and Jerry took their leave, Spud hugged Dani. "Don't be a stranger."

"I won't be."

Spud looked up at Logan challengingly. "Make her promise."

"I'll do my best."

It was deafeningly quiet after the couple left. Dani hadn't noticed that it had grown dark. The summer night was still and crystal clear. She made a monumental task out of straightening the throw pillows that someone had taken from the couch and propped against the stone hearth of the fireplace in the living room. She heard Logan's soft tread as he came up behind her. He took her hand and turned her around.

"Hungry?"

She shook her head. "After all those nachos? No."

"Thirsty?" He answered his own question by mimicking her. "After all those margaritas?" His thumb wrote erotic messages on her wrist. "Drunk?"

"A little," she confessed with a mellow smile.

"Me too." He pulled her close. "But not on tequila."

He kissed her softly with chaste lips. "Feel like a swim?"

"I could stand that." Her smile felt so good against his. Her breasts felt good against his chest. Her body . . . She felt good all over.

"Come on. I've got something even better."

Pulling her through the house, he led her back onto the patio. They crossed the cool stone surface, making their way toward the cabana. A half-moon and a brilliant panoply of stars, which one didn't see in the city, shed silver light and bathed everything in a mystical glow.

Near the back side of the cabana was a high wooden fence. Logan reached above and behind it and extracted a key. He unlocked the gate and swung it open. Winking at Dani, he bowed her through.

"A hot tub!" she exclaimed in delight. The water bubbled and frothed in the redwood tub, which was lit from underneath. It looked like a cauldron of pleasure designed by the most unapologetic of hedonists.

And said hedonist was grinning down at her. "Like it?"

"Who wouldn't? But why didn't you open it for the party?"

"No way. This is only for private parties." He settled his hands on her shoulders and dropped a soft kiss on the nape of her neck. "Need help with this?" he asked, fiddling with the fastener of her halter.

She didn't, but she replied "Please" in a foggy voice.

His capable fingers took an inordinate amount of time undoing the snaps. "I've daydreamed about this a million times, helping you dress and undress. Little husbandly tasks I never got to do."

Ordinarily there would have been nothing suggestive or sensuous about merely fastening a dress. It was the way Logan went about it that left her insides feeling warm and buttery. He pulled the snaps free one by one, delaying the simple process, prolonging the anticipation. When they were all done, he slowly lowered the straps over her shoulders and then helped her slide the dress over her hips. It crumpled in a heap around her feet, leaving her only in her peacock blue strapless bikini.

He slid the coated rubber band down her ponytail until her hair spilled into his hands. It was just as he remembered it—silky, fine, thick, straight, growing from a center part. "I thought you might have cut it."

She shook her head, sending her hair shifting and shimmering over his fingers. "No. I never could bring myself to."

He buried his face in the silken mass. "I'm glad. It's your glory. Isn't that from the Bible or something?"

"It sounds right."

His hands came back to her waist and whispered up and down over the indentation, reshaping it with his calloused palms. "Do you want to take anything else off before you get in?"

For one pulsing moment she leaned against him and let her head fall back onto his chest. Then she remembered. He had issued a challenge. He wanted a wedding night. Was that all this meant to him, repayment of a debt? Didn't she have more pride than to let herself be used this way?

She separated herself from him gently. "Yes." She turned and smiled at him teasingly. "My shoes."

His lopsided grin was wry. "Your shoes weren't exactly what I had in mind."

Sitting on the deck of the tub, she unlaced the

leather cords from around her ankles and took off the sandals. Then she lowered herself into the bubbling hot water. The evening air was cool enough to make it pleasurable. "Oh, Logan, this is wonderful."

He went to a wall unit and dimmed the light in the tub until her body resembled the dancing shadow of a water nymph. He flicked another switch and soft mood music filled the small enclosure whose only ceiling was the star-studded night sky. "Fifteen minutes?" he asked as he adjusted the timer for the agitator.

She rested her head against the deck and looked up at him dreamily. "Ummm. At least."

Their eyes held and her blood became as heated and effervescent as the water caressing her. His eyes were bluer, more intent, than she had ever seen them. Beneath his shelf of brows they blazed down at her.

She watched in hypnotic fascination as his hands went to his waist and yanked free the snap of his shorts. It opened over a tuft of hair that sheltered his navel. Then the zipper was leisurely pulled down. Any remaining lassitude deserted her and her heart began to pound. He couldn't be. He wouldn't.

But he could and he did. The shorts were shoved over his hips, down his muscular thighs, and released. They slithered over bulging calves to his feet.

He was naked. Splendidly, magnificently, carnally naked.

"I'm not ashamed in front of you, Dani," he said quietly as he acknowledged her mute astonishment. "I want you to look at me, to know me. I'm your husband, remember?"

"You *were* my husband," she said gruffly.

"A mere technicality."

As silky as his voice, his body slid into the swirling water. Wantonly the water licked upward, inch by inch, wetting and matting the golden hair, making sleek the bronzed skin. It eddied around his thighs, caressed his loins, spun over his belly. Dani was mesmerized. He was beautiful. Unaccountably, such beauty made her want to lay her hands on him and weep.

Through the surging water he came toward her like a merciless ocean deity intent on satisfying a whim. She shot arrow straight out of the water. Just as automatically, his hands reached out to grab her upper arms and restrain her.

"I still consider you my wife, Dani." He pulled her toward him and the soft collison of their bodies set off a chain of erotic explosions throughout her.

"I'm not your wife, Logan. It was so long ago. Too much has happened to both of us."

"I mean to claim what's mine."

His lips closed over hers as his arms went around her with unarguable possession. He lowered himself to his knees, dragging her back into the whirlpool with him. His hands scaled down her back, over her hips, to stroke the backs of her thighs. Gently he parted them and lifted her against his front. He coaxed her legs to encircle his waist and nestled himself, hard and urgent, in the cove of her thighs.

She was drowning, but not in the swirling water. She was inundated with her own passions. Knowing this wasn't the way it should be, she was powerless against the demands of her own body. For balance, she grabbed handfuls of his hair as he lowered his head and scorched her neck with his lips.

"Logan, please, wait."

"I've waited too long."

He unfastened her bikini top. It was quickly sucked under the surface of the churning water. He gave a glad cry that she involuntarily echoed as her breasts floated against his hair-rough chest.

Her fingers clenched tighter in his hair as his hand found her breast, filled itself with her flesh, fondled her. He rubbed his lips back and forth across the peak until it beaded. Then his lips parted and closed around it. He tugged with such a sweet pressure that she felt it in her thighs and in her womb, as though she were giving birth to love.

But it wasn't love. Not for him. And if she didn't stop him now, there would be no help for her later. "Logan—"

"I want you, Dani." His hand slipped into the bottom of her bikini and squeezed the taut flesh of her bottom.

"Not like this," she moaned. But he was beyond hearing. She pulled his hair painfully until his head came up. "No, Logan," she said raggedly.

His breath was harsh, pumping his chest against hers as he inhaled and exhaled. "Why, Dani?"

"Because I don't want to be a consolation prize for a debt you think you're owed."

"You want me too. Don't try to deny it. I know it. I feel it." He pushed himself higher against her and she swayed in his arms.

Her nails bit into his shoulders as she strove for

control. "It's happening too fast. I didn't know you'd feel this way."

"You knew."

"After ten years? No, I didn't."

"All right. So now you know. What's this coy game?"

"It's not a game."

"Then what is it? I told you last night I wanted a wedding night. All day you've given me reason to believe you would be agreeable. Why did you come back, if not for this? Why didn't you just hightail it back to Dallas?"

Grabbing for reasons like elusive straws, she babbled, "I needed to talk to you about buying some property you own."

Obviously he hadn't expected anything so pragmatic. His head jerked back and he blinked rapidly to bring her into focus. His hands dropped from her hips, and her legs fell from around his. She knelt in front of him, her arms now modestly crossed over her breasts.

"What did you say?" He seemed genuinely baffled.

Dani wet her lips with a nervous, darting tongue. This was the wrong time to bring the subject up and she knew it, but she had no alternative. The fuse of his temper was extremely short now and she dared not delay giving him an explanation.

"I'm . . . I serve on a committee. Friends of Children. Maybe you've heard of it." She paused, glancing at him hopefully, smiling tentatively, but his iron countenance hadn't softened.

"Go on."

"We raise money for physically and mentally

handicapped children. We want to build a summer camp exclusively for them. Your property in Hancock County is perfect for it. Our chairwoman, Mrs. Meneffee, wrote you a letter to that effect a few weeks ago. Since I was coming over here anyway, I volunteered to speak to you about it." She swallowed hard. "Will you sell us the land? Cheaply?"

He remained perfectly still for long moments. The bubbling water and their nakedness now seemed like a tasteless joke. The romance of the night had turned into an obscene parody.

Then he began to tremble. A low rumbling noise like a volcano about to erupt issued from his chest. Suddenly he bellowed and vaulted out of the tub. Reaching down, he closed his fist around her mane of hair and hauled her up with him. Furious, dripping water and rage in equal proportions, he shoved his angry face toward hers. His voice was surprisingly mild. She would have preferred shouting. "You mean that you've been stroking me all day, figuratively and literally, to butter me up? You've been setting me up to ask me for a charitable donation?"

"No!"

"That's sure as hell what it looks like."

"How could you think such a thing?"

"How could I think otherwise? Dammit!"

He paced within the perimeters of the fence, muttering curses and vulgarities that made her ears burn. He whipped a towel from a rack and slung it around his waist, carelessly tucking in the end. Facing her, he let his breath out between his teeth in a soft whistle. "I don't know why I'm so surprised. What else could I have expected from you? Apparently wedding vows don't mean much to you. Does anything, Dani? Do you hold anything sacred and dear?"

Yes! she wanted to scream at him. *A commitment you'd never understand, Mr. Webster.* But she wasn't about to explain it to him, not when he thought her capable of such callousness. She wanted to tear into him, rip his arrogant righteousness to pieces, but it was difficult to show anger when she was dripping wet, covering her breasts with trembling hands.

"The work we do is very important, Logan," she said levelly, coldly. She had begun to shiver.

"I grant you it is, Dani. Do you think I begrudge handicapped kids a summer camp? What bugs the hell out of me is that society dames like you think you can manipulate people."

"I'm not a society dame."

"I read the newspapers, Dani. I see your pictures at all those fund-raising balls and fashion show luncheons and celebrity golf tournaments. Why do I get the impression that you're not thinking as much about the charity you're supporting as you are of getting your picture in the papers?"

"You're a snob, Logan. An inverted snob. Do you think poor people have a monopoly on generosity?"

He went on as though she hadn't spoken. "What do you do, go back to the clubhouse and compare notes with your friends? Do you hold contests to see who gets the biggest grant? Do you collect donations like scalps to hang on your Gucci belts? How far do you go to get the biggest donations, Dani?"

"As far as I have to," she flared.

"I think I've just had a sampling." His eyes dropped significantly to her breasts. "What made you stop? Surge of conscience? Should I cut off a lock of hair for you to take back so your friends will know just how dedicated you are?"

"Forget it, Logan. I'm leaving."

She tried to move past him, but he grabbed her and shook her arms free of her breasts. "Do you want that land, Dani?"

"I said to forget it."

"I asked you a question. Do you want that land?"

"Yes. Will you sell it?"

"No." Humiliated for having asked again, she struggled to free herself. Her efforts did nothing but bring her tighter against him. "But I'll give it to you."

She froze and raised her eyes to his. They were like cool blue glass in the moonlight, as hard and unyielding as his body, as his chest against her breasts, as his thighs against hers. "G . . . give it to me?"

"For a price."

"I thought you said—"

"No money. You know what I want in return."

Sudden understanding brought a soft gasp to her lips. "You mean—"

"A wedding night," he finished. "One whole night in bed. With you. Do you want that land bad enough to give me that?"

Oh, God. He didn't know what he was asking. Hundreds of faces flashed through her mind—faces she couldn't put names to. Beautiful faces, ugly faces, pitiful faces. All looking toward her hopefully. She had committed herself to helping them. They were counting on her. But . . .

To spend one night with Logan. One night. Would she ever be able to leave him after one night? She would have to. She would have no choice. One night. With Logan.

She looked up at him. He was calmly waiting for her answer, showing no emotion. This was still a debt owed him, nothing more. He saw an opportunity to make a good bargain, to get something he wanted in exchange for something she wanted.

But for her, it would be a night of love. She would finally know Logan's love, know the strength and security of his arms. For one night out of her life she wanted to bask in his caresses. To hear his love words whispered in her ears. To feel him inside her, a part of herself.

"All right," she said softly. "You've got a deal. One night with me in exchange for the deed to the land."

She felt the tension ebb out of him, but he didn't release her. Instead he gathered her closer and bent low over her. His breath misted her face. "Let's seal it with a kiss."

He pressed his mouth to hers and her lips opened without any resistance. Her mouth was treated to the lazy inspection of his tongue. It mated with hers, rubbed and stroked and probed until her senses were reeling. The towel slipped unnoticed from his waist. She knew the thrill of warm, hair-dappled skin and the hard velvet of male power as a sweet pressure against her belly.

He lifted her easily into his arms and carried her masterfully across the patio and into the dim house. He marched through the house and up the stairs. They didn't speak, but his gaze, so different from moments ago, was hot as it scanned her face and throat and breasts, still rosy from the water and her own increasing arousal.

She got a vague impression of a spacious bedroom and a wide bed as they crossed the threshold. Then his knee bent and she was lowered onto a soft bedspread. He followed her down and kissed her deeply as his weight settled over her.

He worked the bikini bottoms over her hips and down her slender legs until she lay naked beneath him. He kissed her breasts with his lips, with his tongue, with his mouth. His palms slid up her calves, over her thighs. He came close, closer, so close to what begged to be caressed. Groaning, she arched her back and strained against that rigid promise his body made to hers.

Disengaging her arms from around his neck, Logan suddenly pulled away. He was a lithe shadow as he moved toward the door. "Good night, Dani."

As though hinged at the waist, she sprang out of her impassioned stupor into a sitting position. "What do you mean, good night?"

"Just what I said."

"But I thought . . . the wedding night .   ."

"Oh, I intend to hold you to your bargain. But not tonight. There was no time limit placed on our deal. And until I decide to consummate it . . ."—he grinned—"a most appropriate word under the circumstances . . . you'll stay here with me."

"What! Stay? For how long?"

He shrugged and began to close the door. "Until the mood strikes me."

Four

She fretted, cursed, paced . . . and finally slept.

She was too proud to leave. Just as she was too proud to demand that Logan release her from this ridiculous "deal" he had conceived. She had walked into it with her eyes open and had no one to blame but herself.

To think, the first time she had sold her body and the buyer wouldn't take it! It was too humiliating. So, after several teeth-gnashing hours, she availed herself of the comfortable guest room, climbed between fresh-smelling sheets, and dropped into a disgustingly deep and peaceful sleep.

The sun was well up when she awakened. After orienting herself and remembering the night gone by, she threw off the covers and went in search of something to wear. All she had was the bottom to her bikini. When she faced Logan for the showdown she knew must come, she didn't want a skimpy swathe of spandex to be her only armor.

In the decadently opulent bathroom adjoining the bedroom, she found a thick terrycloth robe hanging on a porcelain hook on the back of the door. She slipped it on, feeling not much more protected than if she had on only her bikini bottoms. It was discomfiting to think of facing Logan any way other than fully clothed.

Tossing back her hair and giving a militant tilt to her chin, she pulled the door open and stalked into the hall. Morning smells, tantalizing breakfast smells, greeted her and she followed them down the stairs and into the sunlit kitchen.

Logan was sitting at the round butcher block table. The ream of paper which made up the Sunday morning edition of the Dallas newspaper was scattered around his chair on the tile floor. He was absently sipping coffee, his bare feet propped on the chair opposite him.

His cutoffs were ragged and raveled. His T-shirt had seen better days. His chin was shadowed with a night's growth of beard. His hair hadn't been brushed.

He looked marvelous.

When he heard her bare feet enter the kitchen, he tipped down the corner of his newspaper. She expected derision, a smug smile, a gloating grin.

She didn't expect him to instantly drop the paper—the sports section yet—stand, walk over to her, and put his arms around her in a gentle hug. "Good morning, love."

His hands moved up to cradle her face and his mouth lowered to hers for what she expected would be a soft, closed-mouth, perfunctory good morning kiss. Again she was surprised.

His mouth settled firmly over hers. His lips parted and nudged hers apart as well. Then his tongue pressed deep into her mouth.

She was furious with him, but she couldn't break off the long kiss. He had stupefied her. If not the passionless good morning kiss, she would have expected a conqueror's kiss, a hard, dominating kiss that would have stamped her as his victory trophy in a contest of wills. But this was the kiss of a lover, tender and sweet and sexual.

When he pulled back at last, he dropped several quick kisses on her lips before he asked, "Did you sleep well?"

His matter-of-fact, we-do-this-every-morning inflection penetrated her daze and she squirmed away from him, pulling the tie sash on the robe tighter around her waist.

"No, I did not sleep well," she cried angrily. "Logan, this game of yours is wearing thin. You can't keep me here—"

"Funny, when I checked on you, you were sleeping like a baby." Disregarding her rigid posture, he pulled her close and nuzzled her ear. "You snore."

"I do not!" Of course she didn't know whether she did or not. It had been years since she had slept with anyone. "But I don't want to talk about snoring. I want to talk about—"

"That's okay though. I like the way you snore. I'm sure you're hungry by now. Sit down. Breakfast is keeping warm in the oven. Coffee or tea?"

Because he had totally ignored her exasperation and turned away to get another cup and saucer out of the pantry, she could only stare after him in mute frustration. "Coffee or tea?" he repeated, glancing at her over his shoulder. His smile was dazzling, disarming, and destructive to every argument she had methodically lined up in her mind. His charm shot them down one by one, like targets in a shooting gallery.

"Coffee," she said crisply. "No sugar. Cream."

"Isn't it funny," he commented as he stirred half and half into her coffee, "that we've been married for ten years but I didn't even know how you like your coffee. That's only one of the things I want to learn about you." He was making promises again, this time with his voice, which stroked her senses like a mink glove. "Sit down," he said, setting her coffee on the table.

"I don't want to sit, Logan. I want to talk."

"You can't talk sitting down?"

"Don't be cute," she snapped. "I can't sit across the breakfast table from you and chat as though nothing has happened."

"Nothing *has* happened," he pointed out with maddening logic. "Believe me, my manhood is achingly certain that nothing has happened."

She ignored the color that rushed to her cheeks and made them warm. "Please appreciate how uncomfortable this makes me."

"Why should you feel uncomfortable?"

"Because I don't have any clothes on, for one thing. I think that puts me at a distinct disadvantage."

"Well, if that's all it is." He reached for the snap of his threadbare cutoffs. "I'll take my clothes off and then you won't feel so much at a disad—"

"No!" She thrust a staying hand out in front of her. Her sudden reaction made his eyebrows spring into perfect arches as he glanced at her, a smile lifting the corners of his lips. "Would you please get my bags from my car? I'd like to dress."

"Your bags have already been brought in. There'll be plenty of time to dress after breakfast. Now sit down." It was a softly spoken command she had no choice but to obey. He reached for her hand, jerked her forward, and gave her a slight push into the chair near his. "Are you hungry?"

She was starving. "No." His benign face darkened perceptibly and she hastened to say, "But you go ahead. I'm not much of a breakfast eater."

He opened the oven door and took out two plates of bacon and steaming scrambled eggs. When he set them before her on the table, her mouth began to water. "Do you like blueberry muffins?" he asked, picking up a bread warmer and placing it beside the other food.

She ignored his question and asked one of her own. "Did you do all this yourself?"

"The eggs and bacon, yes. My housekeeper made the muffins and froze them. I'm good at taking things from the freezer and putting them in the microwave."

"Housekeeper?" She tossed him an arch look. "I seem to recall you scorning maids and such."

"I'm a man living alone. Since I don't have a wife"—he paused to emphasize the last word—"living with me, I have to hire someone to give me tender loving care."

"I thought tender loving care was Lana's department." Hoping he would deny it, she was instead treated to a slow, knowing smile.

"Jealous?"

"Of course not!"

He laughed. "Yes, you are." He gripped a handful of the terrycloth covering her chest, lifted her from the chair, pulled her onto his lap, and kissed her smackingly. He moved her plate next to his and handed her a fork. "I like you better over here. Now eat up."

"What about your housekeeper?" she asked around her first sumptuous mouthful of muffin. "Won't you be embarrassed if she walks in and finds us this way?"

"I gave her a few days off."

"When?"

"I called her this morning."

"So you fully intend for me to stay?"

"You want to, don't you?"

"It's not a matter of *wanting. You* laid down the terms of the bargain."

"*You* could have refused them. But you didn't."

She didn't want to appear too agreeable. "I might reconsider."

"But you won't. You want that property too much."

"Did you ever stop to think that I might have other . . . obligations?"

"Is there someone waiting for your return to Dallas?"

She avoided his eyes. She could lie and say 'yes,' but what good would that do her? He wasn't going to let her go anyway. "No."

"No one?"

"No."

That seemed to please him immensely, but he didn't lord it over her. "For someone who wasn't hungry and isn't much of a breakfast eater, you managed to polish that off nicely." Amused, he nodded toward her empty plate.

"I guess I had more of an appetite than I thought," she confessed ruefully.

"I've got an enormous appetite," he said huskily. The earnestness in his eyes began to stir her even before his lips touched hers lightly. "Didn't you ever get hungry for me, Dani? In the past ten years, didn't you ever think about our kisses and what they felt like, what they made our bodies feel like?"

The soft kisses he was pressing against the corner of her lips made thinking almost impossible, but she managed to whisper, "A few times."

"I think about them all the time. I didn't even kiss you on our first few dates. I was afraid of scaring you off. Then, when I did, I didn't dare open my mouth. But I remember the first time I used my tongue and tasted you for real."

She made whimpering noises that were pleas for him to put action to his words. His lips were teasing hers, preparing them for the gentle assault. When it came, she surrendered to it and crossed her arms behind his neck. She kissed him back, joining him in an orgy of rediscovery.

His mouth released hers at last and moved down the side of her neck. "I used to get hard just thinking about your kisses," he muttered thickly.

"Logan!"

"Don't pretend to be shocked. You're bound to have known."

"Nice girls don't think about such things."

"Liar."

In spite of herself, she giggled, thinking back on all the afternoons when she was supposed to have been studying and instead had occupied herself speculating on Logan's anatomy, daydreaming about him.

His face snuggled between the folds of the robe and his tongue feathered along her collarbone, treating it to delightful, dewy licks. His coarse beard stubble scraped her skin deliciously. "Dani?"

"Hmmm?"

"Have you ever made love sitting in a bentwood chair at the breakfast table?"

"No," she answered in a distracted, smoky voice.

"Well, you're about to if you don't stop rolling your cute little tush across my lap."

"Oh!" she exclaimed, jumping to her feet, her cheeks scalding with fury and shame. "I wasn't." I—"

"Hey!" He stood up and hugged her protesting body against his. "I wasn't complaining. I just thought you ought to be forewarned."

"Well, now I have been." She pushed away from him and tried to assume the stance and expression of a woman in perfect control of herself and the situation. "Would you like me to help with the dishes?"

His lips were twitching with the need to laugh, but he accepted her offer as solemnly as it had been issued.

"That would be very gracious of you. Thank you."

When the dishes were done, he led her up the stairs and into the bedroom across the hall from the one she had slept in. "This is the master suite," he said with a flourish of his hand. It was enormous, with a bed of awesome proportions against one wall and a maze of shelves containing video equipment, stereo components, and books on the other. Two easy chairs formed a sitting area in front of a brass fireplace neatly tucked into one corner. A wall of windows opened onto a view of the sweeping pastureland and east Texas pine forest. From her position near the door she could see into the bathroom. The tub in it made the one in the guest bathroom look like a kiddie pool compared to an Olympic-sized swimming pool.

"What do you think?"

The fur bedspread caught her eye. It was lush, thick, erotic. But she decided that, along with the other masculine touches in the room, it was in perfect taste. "It's . . . very nice."

He grinned good-naturedly. "Do I detect a hesitation?"

"No, no, I really like it. It's just so "—she gestured with her hands—"big."

"I had it designed for two people to share."

"I see," she said quietly.

She sensed in the way he moved closer to her, almost looming over her, that only an iron will kept him from carrying the conversation further. Instead, he said, "Here are your bags." He lifted her two suitcases. "I used the key in your purse to open the car, but I put it back."

"Thank you." That seemed the only thing to say as she picked up her purse and followed him. He deposited her luggage in the guest room. She didn't know if she was relieved or disappointed that he hadn't left them in the master suite.

"I think the bathroom's fairly well stocked, but if you don't find something you need, just ask."

"I will."

He rested one hand on her cheek. With a tender pressure, he drew her face up to his for a bone-melting kiss on her mouth. His lips brushed her cheek, her ear. Then, without a word, he left, closing the door softly behind him.

The luxurious inch-deep pile of the carpet pampered her bare feet. Her breasts were aching and full, as though with milk. Her nipples tingled. Between her thighs was a pulsing heat. Her heart was pounding. She was trembling.

And he had left her alone.

"Damn him and his silly games," she said to the four walls as she angrily strode into the bathroom. As soon as she was showered and dressed in more than this terrycloth robe, she was going to tell him exactly what he could do with the deal he had dreamed up. Then she would leave for Dallas.

But as she entered the bathroom she noticed the bouquet of roses that her sleepy eyes had missed earlier that morning. The lead crystal bowl was filled with perfect yellow buds in the first stages of blossoming and snowy baby's breath as delicate as its namesake. There was a card. It read: *There are incredibly soft places on your sleeping body.*

Her body went hot all over. She had slept naked, having had nothing but the damp bikini bottoms to wear. She had dreamed of him, of his kisses, of his caresses. Had some of those fantasies not been dreams at all, but reality?

Her knees were rubbery and the cold, bracing shower did nothing to strengthen them. She realized she should dress and leave while she still could. But she gazed at the flowers and the card, sighed, and knew that even if she lived to regret it, she was going to stay. For a while longer, at least.

In bra and panties, she sat on the small padded stool before the dressing table. Theater lights surrounded the mirror, making it perfect for applying makeup. Dani wondered how many women had stared at themselves in that mirror, warm and purring contentment after having shared Logan's bed.

The thought hurt, and her face drew into a frown which was quickly replaced by a slack-mouthed gape of astonishment as the door opened behind her. Logan strolled in wearing nothing but a pair of briefs and a broad smile. Apparently he had just showered too. His skin and hair were damp.

"You should have knocked." Instinctively, she splayed a hand over her chest. Her breasts swelled above the low-cut, sheer brassiere. Far from restraining them, it seemed to lift them on a shelf for better viewing.

"Sorry." His grin said remorse was the least of his sentiments. "I've fantasized about this so many times, us married, getting dressed together. It seemed natural to barge right in. However, in none of my fantasies did you try to cover yourself. That's silly, isn't it? I've already seen you."

Irritated by the calm, indifferent way he was leaning against the doorjamb, she lowered her shielding hand and picked up an eyebrow pencil, determined to appear as unperturbed as he seemed to be. "I think you have some deep-seated psychological problem. You have a real penchant for taking off your clothes and parading around virtually naked."

"My deep-seated psychological problem, as you put it, stems from being raised in a four-room house with my parents, a sister, and a brother. There wasn't much room at home for modesty."

She could have bit her waspish tongue. She gazed at him contritely through the mirror. She knew he wouldn't want to discuss his humble beginnings, so she said, "The flowers are beautiful."

"So are you when you're asleep."

She swallowed hard. "Then you did . . . uh . . ."

"Yes."

"And . . . uh . . ."

"That too. I touched you with unspeakable shamelessness." He pushed away from the door and dropped to his knees behind her. He hooked his now shaven chin over her shoulder, laid his cheek against hers, and looked at her in the mirror. His eyes were hazy with desire. "Does my nakedness truly offend you?"

"Truly?" she asked with a soft laugh. "No."

He smiled back, relieved. "Well, yours sure as hell doesn't offend me." His hands stroked downward from her shoulders onto the soft swells of her breasts. Entranced, they both watched his strong, tanned hands cover her. "You feel . . . God, you feel good, Dani."

His touch was sure, firm, warm. The lacy confection of her brassiere was no deterrent. His gentle squeezes plumped her. She filled his palms. Overflowed them. Through eyes growing cloudy with passion, Dani watched his thumbs as they stroked her. Slowly. Rapidly. Back and forth. In circles. Until she became perfectly, beautifully awakened. Then he played with her caressingly.

Her arms went slack; she collapsed backward against his chest; her eyes closed and her lips parted to release staccato puffs of breath. The eyebrow pencil rolled from relaxed fingers and landed soundlessly on the carpet.

"Do you like that?"

"Yes."

"Softer? Harder?"

"No . . . no . . . just . . . just like that."

"Like that?"

"Hmmm."

He whispered outrageous things about her color, her shape. "Delicate and sexy, but maternal. You could entice a lover one moment and nourish an infant the next."

Turning his head, he nudged her with his nose until her face came around to his. With a sweet suction he sealed their mouths together, planting his tongue deep. It slid in and out while his fingers continued to gently pluck, his thumbs to entice, his palms to caress.

Groaning, he dropped his hands and swiveled her around to face him. Hugging her tightly against him, he buried his face in her neck. "You're my wife, Dani. My wife. Do you hear? My wife." For long moments he held her like that, as though he'd never let her go.

When he finally did, they were both embarrassed by their intense emotions. Confounded, she faced the mirror again and replaced her lingerie. He stood behind her and forcibly composed himself. Smiling gently, he pressed the back of her head against his stomach and stroked her jaw until she dared to meet his eyes in the mirror. "I got carried away," he said softly. "I'll let you dress now so we won't be late."

"Late? Are we on a schedule?"

"If you don't hurry, we won't get there by eleven o'clock."

"Are we going somewhere?"

"This is Sunday. We're going to church."

"Couldn't we have sat in the balcony?"

She was speaking out of the side of her mouth, but smiling in order to camouflage her chagrin. Logan had marched her down the center aisle to the third row of the sanctuary.

"This is my regular pew." He nodded a greeting to the passing usher, who heartily shook his hand and handed him an order of service.

"You come here often?"

"Every Sunday," he said piously. "Don't you attend church? Or are you too busy doing good deeds?"

He had teased too hard. He realized it immediately when her face took on a stricken look and her body tensed. "Don't tease me about the work I do, Logan. About anything else, but not about that."

"I'm sorry. I didn't mean to make light of it."

He spoke with such sincerity that she instantly forgave him. She even managed a wavering smile. "In answer to your question, yes, I do attend church regularly."

His mouth twitched with a suppressed smile. "I'm glad you're staying on the straight and narrow."

"You're a hypocrite," she whispered as she busied herself with decorously straightening the hem of her skirt over her knees.

"How's that?"

"I wonder what these good folks would think of the terms of our deal."

"They'd probably think that I'm an extremely clever fellow."

"And what would they think of your piety if they knew I'd spent the night under your roof? Or are they so used to young ladies residing with you that no one would be surprised?"

His eyes were dancing with mischief. "Shhh, the service is starting."

Piqued by his sanctimonious expression, she smuggled her hand between them and pinched his waist. He almost yelped out loud, but covered it with a cough.

As punishment, he grasped her hand and held it throughout the service. It wasn't the worst punishment ever inflicted on her. In fact, there was something uplifting about standing with him, sharing his hymnal, listen to his deep baritone as he sang.

She was proud to be standing beside him. He was such a handsome figure in his dark blue three-piece suit, the cut and fit of it unmistakably hand tailored. His white shirt was crisp with starch, his tie, discreet and tasteful. The French cuffs with their gold-ball cuff links looked startlingly white against his hands and their sprinkling of golden hair. He smelled of soap and cologne and peppermint-flavored toothpaste.

When they bowed their heads in prayer, she knew a spiritual high she had never known before. Every night since she had watched him being shoved into the sheriff's car and out of her life, she had asked God's blessing on him. If she never had another day with him, she would be eternally glad for this moment when he stood so tall and straight and strong next to her.

She inched closer for the reassuring feel of his sleeve against her bare arm. He lifted his arm and draped it across her shoulders. His hand squeezed her shoulder lightly and she knew that his prayers were being lifted toward heaven on the same course as hers.

After the service she was introduced to people she didn't know, and reacquainted with those she had known in her youth. It wasn't hard to tell that Logan was highly respected in the community. He was friendly to everyone. Those who stopped to talk to him basked in the radiance of his smile.

As they were making their way to his car, they were practically tackled by three husky children who hurled themselves enthusiastically against Logan. He greeted them boisterously. Spud came chasing after her brood, the baby straddling her hip and clinging to her shoulder. Jerry, with his easygoing smile, loped behind her like an obedient puppy.

After they had exchanged hellos and Dani had been introduced to the children, Spud asked wickedly, "Well, what have you two been up to? Or don't I know?"

Dani blanched. Logan chuckled. Jerry chastised. "Spud, we're still on church grounds. And the kids," he whispered.

"Well, I want to know," she said defensively. Her eyes were busy darting from Logan to Dani, as though looking for telltale signs of satiation. "Are you going to stay awhile, Dani?"

"Uh . . ."

"Awhile," Logan said smoothly, once again placing a proprietary arm around her shoulders.

"Exactly where are you staying? At the motel?"

"See ya, Jerry, Spud." Logan turned Dani away.

"But . . . but, wait! You haven't told me anything."

"Good-bye, Spud," Logan called over his shoulder. Dani was laughing against his chest.

By the time they reached the car, Jerry was trying to herd his family into the economy-sized station wagon. Spud was still protesting, the baby was squalling, and the children looked like chattering perpetual motion toys out of a housewife's nightmare.

Logan and Dani laughed together as he started the motor. "What'll it be? Sunday buffet at the country club or tuna sandwiches by the pool?"

"Which pool?"

"My pool."

"Tuna sandwiches."

"You have to help make them," he warned.

"That doesn't sound so bad."

She was having a hard time keeping from smiling. Smiles seemed to come so easily. It was that way all afternoon. She didn't remember a sunnier, lovelier day. Her tuna salad was different from his housekeeper's, but he declared he liked hers better. After the light lunch they swam and lolled in the sun. She drowsed on a chaise only to be awakened by his oiled hands stroking the backs of her thighs.

"So you won't burn," he said when she raised her head to look back at him.

"Thank you."

"My pleasure."

It was her pleasure too. His oiled hands glided over her with just the right amount of pressure to make the caress erotic. He touched secret, sensual spots she didn't know she had, until her body was humming with arousal. But it was Logan who muttered a heartfelt oath and dove into the pool to cool off. She knew that his own waiting game was getting to him. It did her heart good to see him suffering, because she felt as though she were floundering in an ocean of consuming fire.

At sundown, when she came back downstairs after a shower, he had lighted charcoal in the outdoor grill. "Shish kebabs?" he asked.

He had showered too. His hair had been carelessly towel dried. The hair on his legs was still damply curled. He was wearing shorts and a thin gauze shirt that was buttoned only half-way. She could detect the swirling patterns of his chest hair and the dark shadows of his nipples.

She smacked her lips, though at the moment she couldn't have sworn it was over the thought of shish kebabs. "Sounds delicious."

"You're delicious," he said in a low, vibrant voice. She wore a loose peach-colored caftan. It was floor length, but had a deep V opening in front, and through the shimmery fabric Logan could see the clear definition of her slender figure. Her ears were adorned with large golden hoops that reminded him of a pagan priestess, but her hair looked like an angel's as it fell to the middle of her back in soft, heavy strands.

"I'll skewer the meat and vegetables if you'll cook the rice."

"That sounds fair."

She also made the salad and blended her own

dressing from the spices she found in his well-stocked pantry. Dipping her finger into the measuring cup, she sampled it.

Logan came toward her and said gruffly, "Let me taste."

Wordless against the fiery glow in his eyes, she dipped her finger into the cup again and lifted it to his lips. First his tongue lightly sponged up the vinegar and oil mixture. "Scrumptious," he murmured. But he clasped her hand to keep it there. His tongue came out again and again to bathe the tip of her finger until he could taste nothing but the unique delicacy of her skin.

Dani was following his every movement, but even so, she wasn't prepared for what he did next. He took her finger between his lips and sucked it inside. His name passed through her lips on a moaning sigh while the liquid heat of his mouth tightly entrapped her finger.

When he finally released it, he drew her close, laid his lips against her ear and whispered, "That's how it'll be for me when I'm inside you, Dani."

Five

For five full minutes it seemed she couldn't breathe. There wasn't enough room in her chest to contain all the emotions that were surging through her. She tried to appear cool, nonchalant, sophisticated, unbent, unmoved, unaffected. Actually, the shocking statement he had made had turned her bones to jelly and her muscles to mush. Each time she looked at him, she knew her efforts to appear aloof were in vain and that her desire was nakedly apparent. His certainly was.

Their dinner conversation was banal. Though they each made an effort at normalcy, they often lapsed into silences rife with tension and restraint. His low, deep voice would diminish to nothingness in mid-sentence. His eyes, shining intensely blue in the candlelight on his dining table, would hungrily wander over her. In his temple ticked a racing pulse that she timed perfectly with hers. She knew he was feeling as warm and languorous as she was.

"Finished?" he asked, indicating her plate.

Glancing down, she was surprised to see that she had eaten almost all her portion, though she didn't remember tasting a thing. "Yes. It was delicious."

"More wine?" Without waiting for her answer, he tipped the chilled bottle toward her goblet and refilled it. "Let's take this out on the patio."

Standing, he eased back his chair and came around the end of the table to help her out of hers. Carrying their glasses of wine and with her hand loosely clasped in his, he escorted her through the house.

"Logan, how lovely!" she cried as they slipped through one of the glass doors. Dozens of votive candles were floating on the surface of the pool.

"You like?"

"Oh, it's . . . it's beautiful. Magic." The tiny flickering flames looked like fireflies dancing on the mirrored surface.

He led her to the side of the pool and worked his feet out of his topsiders. He sat down, pulling her with him, and lowered his feet into the water. After sliding off her sandals, she did the same. She draped the caftan's hem over her lower thighs. They watched the rippling shadows of light and water marbleize their skin. His toes came up to stroke her high arch.

Turning to look at her, he raised his glass. "To honeymoons that come ten years late." Smiling, she clinked her glass with his and they sipped the full-bodied wine.

"Why do you say that?"

With his free hand he fiddled with her earring. "About delayed honeymoons?"

"Yes."

"I doubt you'd have been this relaxed a bride ten years ago. I counted on several nights of feeling like a sex-crazed beast until I could woo you into liking the 'marital act.' "

She was shocked. "Is that what you thought?"

"Isn't that how it would have been?"

"No. I wouldn't have been like that at all." It was his turn to be surprised and he peered at her closely. She lowered her eyes demurely. "I mean, I was a little frightened, but not of you. Only of the unknown, of losing my virginity. But I was eager to . . . to make love to you, Logan."

"Obviously not as eager as I was to make love to you."

She stared out over the enchanting setting he had arranged for her benefit. "I think if we talk about that, we'll argue. And I don't want to argue with you. Not tonight. The day has been too perfect."

"You're right. Let's talk about something else." They fell into a lengthy silence while they finished their wine.

At last he turned toward her and continued staring at her profile until she looked back at him. "I can't think of anything else to talk about. Could you get into some heavy petting?" he asked solemnly.

She sputtered a laugh at his deadpan sincerity, but drew her face into a facsimile of his seriousness. "I'm not that kind of girl."

"Oh, hell." He looked properly crestfallen. "Still?"

She let her gaze drift downward toward his

mouth and her eyes glowed with a deliberately sultry expression. "Don't give up so easily."

That was all the encouragement he needed. He promptly stood and pulled her up with him. He led her to the glider, sat down, and drew her onto his lap for the second time that day. With a sustained pressure on her shoulder, he pressed her into the corner cushions until she was lying across his chest, her bottom snug in his lap, her thighs draped over his. He leaned over her.

"Comfy?"

She cupped the back of his head with a caressing hand. Her fingers tangled in his hair, then slid around his neck to explore the high cheekbones, the hard ridge of his jaw, the length of his nose, the cleft in his chin. When she touched his lips, his breath hissed softly against her fingertips.

Willfully, but beseechingly, his mouth came down on hers. His kiss demanded her lips to part, but once inside, his tongue dipped into the sweet inner recess with tender appreciation. His hand went exploring and was rewarded. He sighed his pleasure in what he found.

"No bra tonight?"

"No."

"Why didn't you go without when we were dating?"

"I remember a few times when you managed to get past it." Coyly she ducked her face into his neck.

"God, so do I," he groaned. "But it makes things so much easier without all the snaps and hooks. I think they were designed solely to frustrate me."

Her soft laugh was captured by his mouth. Again and again he kissed her, while his hand fondled her through the thin cloth of her caftan. Her neck and throat were covered with moist kisses. His fingertips fanned her nipple lightly until it tightened.

"Sweet, sweet." Lowering his head, he covered the tip of her breast with his mouth. He nudged the flushing flesh with his tongue, raked it gently with his teeth.

Tiny floodgates gave way inside Dani, releasing pent-up passion that flowed through her like honey. Her fingers threaded through his hair. "Logan, Logan, you make me burn."

"Where, love?"

"All over. Everywhere. My breasts."

"Where else?"

His hand slipped beneath the hem of the caftan and caressed the satiny length of her thigh. The sound she made deep in her throat was born of both gratification and longing. He massaged her stomach, pressing slow circles into her flesh with his flattened palm. His fingertips strummed over the triangle of her panties repeatedly, robbing her of a little more breath each time.

"Here?" he whispered.

"Yes, yes."

To save his sanity, he pressed his forehead to hers and stilled his hand. It molded to the curve of her hip as his thumb rotated over her hipbone. "Nothing in the world feels like your skin."

"Did you really touch me last night while I was asleep?"

"Yes. Not as much as I wanted to."

"I felt it."

"Did you?"

"I thought I was dreaming."

"I thought I was too."

They kissed with unleashed passion, their mouths hungry, twisting together. When he pulled back, he asked, "Are you ready to go upstairs?"

She nodded, and he lifted her off his lap and set her on her feet. She swayed against him and he wrapped his arm around her waist. They didn't speak, not even when they reached the door to the guest room. His arms closed around her possessively and he kissed her with fierce ardency.

She glued her body to his, arching against his hardness, cradling it between her restless thighs. The muscles in his arms bunched as he hugged her tighter. And when he pulled back to look down into her face, her eyes shimmered up at his.

"You'd better get some sleep. Good night."

She couldn't believe it! He was actually dropping his arms and turning away from her, heading for the top of the stairs. "Where are you going?" she asked with a mortifying absence of pride.

"To do the dishes."

"The dishes! You mean you're not going to . . . to . . ."

"Not going to what?"

Her nails curled painfully into her palms. Fury stiffened her spine and her chin lifted several inches. She couldn't tell him what she thought their foreplay was leading to without making a fool of herself. And he knew it, and she knew he knew she knew it. "Nothing," she said sharply. "Good night."

She slammed the door to the guest room behind her. "Damn him! He can't do this to me. I refuse to let him. What does he think I am, a mechanical doll he can turn off and on at will?" She stamped across the room, throwing off her clothes. Her footsteps could be heard even in the thick carpet as she paced. "I'm leaving."

She strode into the bathroom and began snatching up everything belonging to her and cramming it into her suitcase. But it occurred to her that if she left in a fit of temper now, he would know how much she cared that he hadn't taken her to bed. She paused and slumped down on the small vanity stool, her energy and rage spent.

She had made a bargain and she must stick to it. As he had so clearly stated, she was on his turf, and his rules applied. If she left now, she would sacrifice not only what scraps of pride remained to her, but also the camp that meant so much to so many.

Sighing, she pulled on a nightgown and went to bed. Lying alone between the sheets in the still darkness, she cursed him again for bringing on the fever in her body. It showed no signs of abating.

Logan, leaning forward slightly, his head hanging between his shoulders, braced himself against the countertop. His uneven breathing rattled harshly in his chest. "You stupid, stubborn idiot," he muttered to himself.

He squeezed his eyes shut against the pain. How long before the fire in his loins cooled and the throbbing pressure subsided?

The dull thuds of her angry footsteps reached his ears from overhead. She was mad as hell and he couldn't blame her. No doubt she thought he was playing some diabolical game. Did she think he

was teasing her, testing her, paying her back for
the torment he had suffered those nights he'd
spent in jail when he should have been honey-
mooning with his bride?

No, Dani, no, his heart groaned, *that's not the
reason I'm not with you now.* What sane man
would impose this kind of physical torture on himself for any reason? Then why the hell was he doing
it? What was he waiting for? Proclamations of
love? Promises?

Okay, yes. But . . .

Dani was in his house. In his bed. Dani. His
Dani. She had been melting with desire. She had
pressed against him so invitingly that only a fool
would back away. Her mouth had been openly
receptive to his kisses. Her arms, her breasts, her
softness . . .

He clawed through his hair with both hands.
"Why didn't you just take it?" he asked himself
aloud.

Because then their deal would be finalized. He
couldn't take a chance that she would leave when
she got the deed to that land. God, he wanted to
take her to bed. But he wanted more. And until he
knew he could have it all, he would just have to
swelter in this private hell.

Dani tried to flick away whatever it was that was
tickling her earlobe.

"This is as soft as the rose's petals."

She forced her eyes open. Sunlight was stream-
ing through the sheer drapes on the wall of
windows opposite the bed. The warm presence

beside her was lulling and comforting. Snuggling closer to it, she yawned and closed her eyes again.

Then she felt the moist, prowling tongue around her ear and the capricious, caressing lips on her neck. Rolling over, she determinedly shook herself into total consciousness. "What are you doing here?"

"I live here." A dazzling smile broke over his face. He was dressed. But reclining next to her, propped up on one elbow, he looked for all the world like a lazy decadent despot with nothing better to do than toy with one of his concubines.

"And your guests have no right to privacy?"

He twirled the rose he'd been tickling her with and sniffed it before laying the petals against her cheek and trailing it down into the opening of her nightgown. "You're still mad."

"I'm not mad!" Her tone contradicted her words.

"Were you that upset I didn't sleep with you last night?"

"Of course not." She wished he would move off the bed. His superior weight made the mattress sink, and she kept sliding against him unwillingly. Each time she touched him, it became more difficult to find the willpower to move away.

He caught a handful of her hair and studied the strands as he rubbed them between his fingers. "Dani, are you that anxious to fulfill the terms of our deal and leave?"

She stopped trying to put space between them. It was futile anyway, because he had tossed the rose aside and his hand was now lying heavily upon her thigh. Even through the covers she could feel its heat.

Stubbornly, she refused to answer his question.

No, that wasn't her reason for wanting him to make love to her. She wanted that with or without a deal. Couldn't he see that? If he couldn't, she wasn't about to enlighten him. She had some pride left.

He touched her cheek. His thumb moved back and forth over her lower lip. "I haven't taken you to bed yet because I wanted to woo you. I wanted it to be the consummation of something more than a business deal. I wanted you to come willingly, because you wanted to."

If she'd been any more willing last night, she would have dissolved into a puddle on his expensive carpet. Could she believe he was holding back for a noble reason, or was he even now dallying with her because of his own perverse motives?

"Aren't you having a good time here with me?" His fingers tugged playfully at her earlobe.

"Yes," she admitted grudgingly.

"Well, I have another big day planned today. Dress in something casual. Jeans, perhaps?"

"I brought a pair."

"Good. I'll leave you now to get ready."

"Where are we going?"

Logan got off the bed and crossed to the door. "I thought you might want to look over the property you've bartered your body for."

She couldn't be offended. He looked so devastatingly handsome when he smiled. He winked devilishly on his way out the door.

She scrambled out of bed and rushed to dress. A half hour later she joined him in the kitchen dressed as he had prescribed, in a pair of jeans and an oversized cotton shirt with wide sleeves rolled to her elbows. She had tied its long tail into a knot at her waist. Her hair had been pulled into a ponytail. "Don't I pass muster?" she asked after the lengthy inspection his eyes subjected her to. He was frowning.

"You'll do."

"What does that mean?" she asked testily, placing her hands on her hips.

"It means that even dressed casually, you still look like something out of Sakowitz's catalogue."

She was inordinately pleased with his reverse compliment and accepted the cup of coffee he brought her with a soft kiss on his cheek. "What's that for?"

Her smile was as sunny as the morning. "For thinking I look nice even casual, Grumpy."

"You're not casual. *This* is casual."

He stood back and spread his arms wide. She took in the soft cotton western-style shirt, the tight—arousingly tight—faded jeans with their frayed hems, and the scuffed cowboy boots which were stained with mud and substances she thought better not to identify. He looked wonderful and her sizzling eyes told him so.

"God, when you look at me like that, I go a little crazy." Grabbing her, he pulled her forward and kissed her thoroughly. His hard body bent over hers, straining to touch, to penetrate. She moved against him.

With a groan he released her and stepped away. "If we keep that up—pun intended—we'll never get away from here. Can you manage to wolf down another half dozen of those blueberry muffins?"

"Only a half dozen?" she asked saucily.

"That's all the breakfast you're going to get." He turned away to fix her a plate and she smiled secretly. He was putting on a good act of cool control, but his body was smoldering on the inside. Knowing how restless she had been before finally dropping off to sleep last night, she wondered what Logan's restraint had cost him.

"Ready?" he asked a few minutes later. Nodding, she blotted up the last crumbs of the muffins and licked them from her finger. Watching her, he laughed and smacked her soundly on the fanny as she passed him going out the back door.

They had driven to church in a sleek silver Seville. Today their transportation was a blue-and-white Ford pickup that had seen its share of hard miles. "Your carriage awaits, Princess. This will be an experience you can tell your Dallas society friends about."

"It's very chic to drive a pickup these days," she said loftily.

They were in a teasing mood and laughed together as he steered the pickup down the lane toward the highway. She knew the general direction they would take to reach the property in Hancock County, but he took a circuitous route, proudly showing off his varied business interests. They drove past the lumber mill that her father's company had once owned and now belonged to Logan. He showed her commercial buildings downtown that he leased out to businessmen. They drove through heavily wooded forests that he held deeds to and sprawling pastureland dotted with impressive herds of Hereford cattle.

At last he turned off onto a narrow farm-to-market road that eventually dwindled to little more than a rutted dirt path. "See why we needed the pickup," Logan said as they stopped before a rustic barbed wire gate. Dani jumped out to open it and Logan drove the pickup through. A half mile beyond that they came to the deserted church camp.

"Logan, it's wonderful!" she exclaimed, once again hopping from the cab of the truck.

His look was plainly incredulous. To his eye the dilapidated buildings looked anything but wonderful. "The place looks like hell," he said bluntly.

"Oh, but so much can be done. Yes, yes," she said eagerly, taking his hand and dragging him forward. "That old chapel would make a great recreation and crafts room. And that building over there must be the dining hall. Let's go see the dormitories."

They spent the next hour exploring the buildings, which hadn't been occupied by two-legged animals in years, but had housed a variety of four-legged creatures. The swimming pool was culturing every species of fungi. The athletic fields were waist high in weeds. Dani was enthusiastic, Logan wary.

"What were you going to do with it?" she demanded, vexed by his lack of vision and imagination. She refused to let him dampen her spirits.

"Nothing but let the land appreciate in value. I could have sold it for a huge profit in a few years' time, even if I never turned a hand. Are you sure you can make a go of this place?"

"With donations for building materials, yes. A lot of elbow grease. Oh, Logan, I love it."

She hugged him and then chased off to do more exploring. "I can't wait to get started," she said, looking back through the rear windshield of the pickup after Logan had finally coaxed her to leave.

"I want it ready by next summer so we can start the camping program then."

He studied her for a long moment. "This means a great deal to you, doesn't it?"

Her head came around and her effervescence momentarily fizzled. "A great deal," she said with heartfelt sincerity. "Does that surprise you so much, Logan? How can you claim to have loved me once and think me too shallow to do something worthwhile for handicapped, and often underprivileged, children without having an ulterior motive?"

"It's not that I think you're incapable of pity—"

"It's not pity. I approach the work practically, not emotionally. It's a job someone needs to do and I'm doing it."

"I find it hard to reconcile the fact that a girl who had your upbringing, who came from the privileged classes, can identify with an economically deprived, retarded child. Especially to the extent of your involvement. Writing out a check, yes. But not taking on a project of this scope, actually getting your hands dirty."

"Some of them aren't economically deprived. Some come from very wealthy families. Spina bifida and Down's syndrome don't recognize class distinctions."

"Is that a subtle put-down meaning that I do?"

"If the shoe fits . . ."

"I'm sorry, Dani." He braked at the gate and turned to face her. His smile was self-deprecating and apologetic. "You're right, I guess. I'm an inverted snob."

"I like you anyway." She reached out to touch his hair.

Leaning forward, he settled his mouth against the corner of hers. "I have a ferocious appetite." She made a small murmuring sound of concession. "How about lunch?"

"Lunch!" She acted affronted and shoved him away.

"You don't expect me to be romantic on an empty stomach, do you?"

"That *is* asking a lot of a big, strapping boy like you, I suppose. But what did you have in mind for dessert?"

"I'd love to discuss that with you," he said, consulting his gold wristwatch, "but if we don't hurry, we're going to be late."

He drove to another remote spot. "Where are we?" Dani asked as he helped her out of the truck. "I thought we were—Is that a horse?"

Logan tilted his head from side to side as he assessed the thoroughbred animal tied to the lower branches of a tree. "My opinion would be that that is definitely a horse. Strictly my opinion, you understand."

"Oh, you!" She swatted the air in front of his face and then went toward the horse. It was bridled, but didn't have a saddle. "How did he conveniently get tethered out here in the middle of nowhere? With a picnic basket, no less, at his feet."

"I've got very good people on my payroll."

She glanced around, seeing no trace of another human being. "I haven't seen any employees."

"That's why they're good," he said, leering. "They're supposed to be invisible. I wanted this to be just like in the movies. You know, where picnic baskets appear from nowhere and violin music pours from the heavens. That kind of thing."

She bit her lower lip to keep from laughing out loud. As had been his intention, she was thoroughly charmed. "But these magician employees forgot something. There's only one horse."

"On the contrary, those were my instructions. You have to ride with me."

"I see." She glanced toward the horse. Crossing her arms over her chest, she played devil's advocate. "Who's going to keep me on, riding bareback?"

His grin was pure, undiluted lechery. "The way I plan to hold you, you couldn't possibly fall off."

"And the picnic basket?"

"You're in charge of it. That way your hands will be occupied while mine are busy—"

"Keeping me from falling off," she finished for him.

He shrugged unrepentantly. "Something like that."

Within minutes they were riding through the sun-dappled woods toward an unspecified destination. She didn't care where they were going. As he had promised, Logan guided the well-trained mount with the merest pressure of his knees, leaving his hands free to roam at will. She protested his audacious caresses, but not too much, not enough to make him stop.

They came to a grassy clearing surrounded by stately pines. In its center stood an enormous pecan tree with sprawling branches. Lifting her down, Logan first spread the blanket, which had been packed in the basket. Then he began to take out their lunch.

It was no ordinary, run-of-the-mill picnic. They ate buttery chicken breast sandwiches on sesame seed rolls, potato salad, olives and pickles, and deviled eggs. For dessert, they had flaky shortbread cookies full of walnuts. They washed it all down with white wine that Logan's "fairy godmother" had left in a cooler behind the pecan tree.

"You're wrong." Dani sighed with satisfaction as she leaned back against the tree. "This is better than in the movies."

"Is it?"

"Much better. They never eat this well in the movies."

She popped one last olive into her mouth and chewed it lazily as she studied Logan stretched out on the blanket. Her brain was fuzzy, but her senses were alarmingly clear. She suspected she was more than a little tipsy on wine and sunshine and Logan. She didn't fight the sexy lassitude that overtook her. It felt too good to wish away. "If you're this well fed all the time, why don't you get paunchy?"

He patted his flat stomach. "You think I'm in pretty good shape?"

She scooted closer to him and impishly tugged at his shirttail until it came out of the waistband. Then she lifted it and peeked underneath. "You look fairly fit," she said jokingly. But when her gaze moved upward to collide with his, her breath caught. There was no teasing gleam in Logan's eyes, only an intense burning light.

"Touch me, Dani." His hands were folded under his head, but his gravelly voice was more compelling than physical force.

It made her afraid, because her own desire to touch him was just as great. She shook her head no, her eyes never leaving his. Earlier, at his request, she had shaken her hair out of the ponytail. Now the sun's rays were trapped in it. She could feel its heat on her back. Or was it her own rising body heat that was making her so warm?

"Touch me," he repeated hoarsely. "How far will you go, Dani?" It was a challenge she couldn't refuse.

Her insides were in turmoil, but she composed her features and laid her hands on his chest. She rubbed them up and down over the hard contours several times. Then, fastening her gaze on his, she began to undo the buttons of his shirt by feel alone.

The backs of her fingers made electrifying contact with the hair-blurred skin. He was so warm, so alive. Even lying perfectly still, he exuded a masculinity that was palpable. She tasted it in the back of her throat. It eked through her fingertips, filled her bloodstream, and found willing targets in the feminine parts of her body. Her nipples pouted. Between her thighs there was a swelling ache.

When all the buttons were undone, she peeled back the shirt. Despite her affected indifference, a murmur of approval escaped her. He was so very pleasing to look at. The soft, crinkly texture of his body hair beckoned her, but not until she saw her hands moving over him and felt the hair's feathery caress against her palms did she realize she had actually heeded the temptation to touch.

The hair fanned out over his broad, muscled chest. She combed through it with rapacious fingers, followed the hard curve of his breast, and absorbed the warmth of his skin and the beating of his heart with pressing palms.

His nipples were dark and flat, but when her fingertips glanced over them, they puckered and hardened in instantaneous response. He gasped, and when she looked at his face, she saw that his jaw was rigid and his eyes were closed.

"Do you want me to stop?" she whispered.

"God, no. Drive me to distraction, Dani. I want you to. Make me delirious with desire for you."

All right, she would. She determined then that he would end this glorious afternoon by making love to her. Putting aside the last of her inhibitions, she lowered her head. Her hair touched him first. Like a silk scarf, it sifted over him. He took handfuls of it in his fists and groaned as though in agony.

Timidly her lips took their first taste. They danced over his throat and chest, sweeping soft, airy kisses that were of little substance, more breath than flesh. Then they found his nipple. She paused. Dare she test its texture against the tip of her tongue as she hungered to? She dared.

"Oh, God!" he breathed.

"Is that good or bad?"

Any other time the tremulously asked question would have alerted him, but he was beyond reasoning through anything. He only gripped her hair more tightly. "Ah, it's good, Dani. So damn good."

She laid her cheek on his stomach. It seesawed beneath his ribcage with each heavy breath. Her lips nibbled along that entrancing strip of brown-gold hair that bisected his middle and furled again around his navel. Her breath drifted over him like a fine mist only a heartbeat before she delicately probed the dimple with her tongue. Emboldened, she stayed to tease with whimsical flicks of her tongue. The unprecedented caress was as arousing to her as it was to him.

She squeezed her eyes closed. She had always wanted to touch him, but had lacked the nerve. That part of him that proclaimed him male had always intrigued her, but it remained a mystery. Now she wanted to discover the very essence of his maleness, to be acquainted with the source of his strength and vitality.

Her hand slid down over his belt buckle to the fly of his jeans. His breath was suddenly suspended. Bravely, she let her hand rest on the hard distension. Tense moments ticked by. Then she gathered all her nerve and slowly curled her fingers around him. At the same time she planted a hot, wet kiss just above his waistband.

His rasping words were either a curse or a prayer. His hand moved down to cover hers. He rubbed the back of it. "You've done it, Dani." He struggled to a sitting position. Cupping her face with his hands, he said hoarsely, "You've driven me over the brink. I can't wait any longer. Let's go home."

Six

They rode back to his house in silence. Logan looked ready to explode. Dani dared not touch him or say anything that might ignite the fuse. His self-imposed restraint was visible. He was so tense, he seemed to have expanded, testing the ability of his clothes to contain him.

"I thought we'd have a late dinner." He unlocked the front door and ushered her in before him.

She turned. His eyes were fairly smoking. "That's fine. I'm not hungry."

"I'll . . . I have some things to do down here before . . . Why don't you go on up and I'll join you?"

"All right, fine."

He touched her cheek. "I won't be long."

As she was making her way upstairs she suddenly knew she would leave. Now. Before anything happened. She closed the door to the guest room and leaned against it, wondering where she would get the strength to leave him again. The thought filled her with anguish. She pressed her fists to her temples.

Oh, she wanted to stay. She wanted to lie with Logan and share with him not only her body, but all the love she had retained for ten years.

Her heart and soul could belong to him if he wanted them. It wouldn't be a passing fancy, a shooting star that would shine brilliantly for an instant before burning itself out. Once she knew the splendor of loving Logan, she would never want to give him up. But she would have to. Logan had his life here. She had hers in Dallas.

There was no sacrificing that, not even for Logan.

But how could she bear to leave him, his passionate loving, his tenderness and warmth and gentleness? Or would he be tender and warm and gentle after his passion was satisfied?

Wasn't she being terribly naive? Logan wouldn't have such an idealistic view of their loving. He was no longer the fresh-faced young Romeo, fervently and eagerly in love with his Juliet. He was no longer the bridegroom anticipating the wedding night when he would make his virgin bride his wife.

He had known countless women. He took them and spurned them as the mood suited him. For him, this wouldn't be an act of love, but only the payoff for a debt long owed him. If he truly loved her, why hadn't he slept with her before now? Did it stand to reason that he would pull back time and again, restraining his own passion, if he wasn't maliciously playing with her, fattening her up for the kill as if she were one of his corn-fed Herefords?

Well, she wasn't a dumb animal to be led blissfully ignorant to the slaughter! Dani felt her heartache giving way to anger, and she welcomed it. Anger would give her the impetus she needed to do what she must. Gathering up her things and shoving them into her suitcases, she fueled her actions with bitterness.

Surely Logan wouldn't bargain over the well-being of unfortunate children? He would eventually see their foolish deal for what it was. She would give him time to cool off before contacting him again. If he didn't come around to selling her the property, property he wasn't even using, then she didn't know him at all.

Dani didn't want a confrontation. Even now she might change her mind if she saw him. When she had finished packing, she opened the door carefully and listened. She heard nothing. Creeping down the stairs and through the house, she ignored the twisting pain in her heart. She didn't think of the man she was leaving. She only concentrated on making good her escape from him without creating a scene.

What does a gentleman wear to a lady's boudoir in the late afternoon? Logan wondered. He had gone to the cabana, choosing to shower there rather than in the master suite. He was afraid that if he came that close to Dani again, he wouldn't be able to stop himself from barging in on her and spoiling the romantic interlude he was planning.

He smiled to himself as he pulled a pair of cotton

pool pants with a drawstring waist from his closet in the cabana. Dani was probably wondering what to wear too. Would she chose a negligee? A simple nightgown? Or would she be waiting for him under the sheets wearing nothing at all?

That thought brought a sheen of perspiration to the body that had so recently stepped from the shower. To cool off, he splashed cologne over his face and throat and chest. He remembered how her lips had felt moving over him and his hand shook as he impatiently raked a brush through his damp hair.

Had he given her enough time? Was she frantically hoping he wouldn't join her until she was ready? Or had he waited too long? Was she wondering what the devil was keeping him? He wanted everything to be perfect. No groom he'd ever heard of had had to wait ten years for his wedding night.

He went to the refrigerator, kept conveniently stocked with beer and soft drinks for poolside guests. Now it was crowded with roses he had had the florist deliver the morning before. He plucked one perfect bud from the vase, then lifted a magnum of champagne from the shelves in the door. He assessed it and, grinning, took out another. "It might be a long night and I intend to work up a powerful thirst," he whispered.

His hands were so slippery with nervousness, he almost dropped the heavy bottles as he stepped out of the cabana and started across the patio. He felt foolish. He was acting like a kid, an innocent groom going to claim an innocent bride. He was actually, amusingly, anxiety-ridden about his performance. But his silliness was excusable because he was in love. And people in love tended to act a little—

He stopped dead still. He didn't even notice the scorching sun-heated tiles burning the soles of his bare feet. Disbelief had rendered him all but senseless. He saw Dani walking briskly toward her car, carrying her suitcases and purse. Even as quickly as she moved, there was an air of stealth about her. He watched as she unlocked the door, thrust her suitcases carelessly inside, and followed them with hurried, jerky motions. The car's motor grumbled to a start. Gravel crunched under the turning wheels. He watched her drive away, leaving a cloud of dust in her wake.

He didn't call after her. He didn't take a single step of pursuit. He didn't move. Everything in him seemed to have died, atrophied. Condensation began to form on the bottles of champagne. The rose began to droop beneath the western sun's blazing heat. And still he stood, watching the dust settle.

People had seen Logan Webster's eyes glisten coldly with anger, crinkle warmly with humor, and cloud with compassion. No one had ever seen them as they were now, swimming with tears.

Without removing the cold compress from her eyes, Dani searched for the ringing telephone. She found the receiver, juggled it, and finally succeeded in bringing it to her ear.

"Hello?" Unless it was Logan calling her to come back, declaring his undying love, she wasn't interested in talking to anybody. It wasn't Logan. It was Mrs. Meneffee calling from Dallas.

"My dear, I've been worried about you. I expected you back days ago."

"I'm sorry. I should have called."

"Nothing wrong, I hope. Car trouble?"

God, her head hurt. Each hair follicle was like a pinprick straight into her brain. Her eyes burned. Her heart ached. It protested each beat as though it wished it didn't have to make the effort. "No, nothing's wrong. I decided to stay for a while, that's all."

"I've been calling your room for days." There was just the slightest hint of reproach in her strident voice. Any other time, Dani would have bristled at this subtle invasion of her privacy. Now, she was too apathetic to care.

"I've been staying with friends," she said vaguely, "and only decided to return to the motel tonight."

"We're all anxious to know. Have you seen Mr. Webster?"

Logan playing volleyball. Logan in the hot tub, water lapping at his naked skin. Logan across the dining table with candlelight reflected in his eyes. Logan stretched out on the blanket under the tree, the filtered sunlight catching in his golden hair. "Yes, I've seen him," she said huskily.

When she didn't expound, the other woman let her exasperation show. "And?"

"And I mentioned the property."

"Well, what did he say, Dani? Are you going to make me beg you for information?"

"I'm sorry. I have a terrible headache. I was napping when you called, so forgive me if I'm fuzzy." She lied adroitly, but her mind was in a tailspin. What was she going to tell Mrs. Meneffee? How could she soften the truth, that she had failed miserably?

"Oh, I'm sorry, dear. If it weren't imperative that I call you, I would have waited until you got back to speak to you."

"Why imperative?"

"Friends of Children is going to make an appeal to a local industry tomorrow for a donation. We want to put our best foot forward. If I could drop a few important names of people who have already contributed to our cause, it might spur them to be more generous."

"Oh, I see." Damn. She would have to give Mrs. Meneffee the bad news tonight. And when she asked why Logan Webster hadn't been cooperative, what was Dani going to tell her?

"By the way, Dani, I went to the after-school day care center today." Barely a year earlier Dani had organized the center to help families with retarded children. The children now had a well-run, cheerful place to go after their special classes so their mothers could work to supplement family incomes. "All I had to do was mention your idea about the summer camp and everyone became ecstatic, parents and teachers alike."

"Oh, I wish you hadn't done that! It's too premature to publicize. I don't want everyone to be disappointed if it doesn't come about." She could easily have wrapped the telephone cord around Mrs. Meneffee's double chins and strangled her.

"Oh, Dani my dear, that's one reason we love and appreciate you so. You work tirelessly, yet don't want to take any of the credit. You're far too modest. I know you'll pull it off. Getting Mr. Webster to consent to sell his land to us is only the first step. What did he say?"

For a fleeting instant she wished that all her other projects hadn't been so successful. So many people were counting on her to come through again. She would just have to come up with an alternative. Maybe she could talk her father into releasing some of his undeveloped property.

"Well, Dani? Have you gone back to sleep? What did he say?"

"He—he didn't exactly say no," she hedged.

"Marvelous. I knew we could count on you. I must go now. Good-bye."

Dani wearily replaced the telephone in its cradle. She hadn't told a lie, but it hadn't been the truth either. She planned on returning to Dallas tomorrow. As soon as she arrived she would have to set things right. She would invent a story about Logan and come up with an alternate plan that would satisfy the committee and wouldn't disappoint the children and their families.

As she got up to pull on a nightshirt, her shoulders felt heavy with responsibility. But no part of her was as heavy as her heart. As she slipped back into bed she wondered if she would have been better off not coming back to Hardwick. She had snubbed her nose on fate by returning to see Logan again. The lesson had been hard learned, but now she knew. Some things were better left alone.

The lock on her door rattled and her eyes opened. It was morning. Light was peeking around the edges of the typically shabby motel drapes. Dani rolled to her side and watched as the door was pushed open. But it had opened no more than a wedge before the chain lock caught it.

"Maid?" she asked groggily. "Later, please."

Just then the chain snapped under the kicking thrust of a booted foot. Its screws were ripped out of the soft wood of the doorjamb, leaving it dangling uselessly. Logan stormed into the room.

"No, it's not the maid. And as for later, what I came for won't be delayed a minute longer."

Dani bolted upright and started to leap from the bed. "Don't bother." The steely voice paralyzed her. "You're right where I want you."

He slammed the abused door shut and stalked into the room. There was no need to speculate on his mood. He was furious, literally quaking with rage. The muscles of his face and neck and arms were rigid with suppressed fury. His eyes were shooting off sparks. He had the bearing of a Viking warlord bent on exacting his due.

Dani brought the covers up to her chin, dimly realizing that even if they were made of iron, they wouldn't shield her from him. "What do you mean by this? You can't come—"

"I can and I have."

She couldn't argue that. He was standing at the foot of the bed now, glaring down at her and making her feel small and unprotected.

"I demand an explanation for this, Logan. Now." She tried to appear coldly courageous, but she was quivering on the inside. She had never seen him, she had never seen *anyone*, in this fierce a mood. And why was he looking at her as though he hated her? Because she had walked out on him? If so, why hadn't he come after her last night?

"Not that you need an explanation," he snarled.

"But read it for your own satisfaction, then I'll take what you've owed me for a long time."

He snatched a sheet of newspaper from his hip pocket and flung it down at her. Still staring at him in bewilderment, she spread it open. Finally tearing her gaze from Logan's, she saw that she was holding part of this morning's Dallas paper. The society section.

She saw the file picture of herself, read the headline and the first few lines of the story, and she knew she was sunk.

"I didn't tell them this," she whispered, her eyes rapidly scanning the page. Each line was a glowing account of her charity work, though under the circumstances it read like an accusation. Her last accomplishment was touted to be the acquisition of some property from Mr. Logan Webster of Hardwick to be used as a summer camp.

At last she laid the paper aside and imploringly looked up at her accuser. "I didn't give them that story. I *didn't*."

"Do you expect me to believe they're clairvoyant?" he roared.

"She . . . she called here last night."

"Who?"

"The chairwoman, Mrs. Meneffee. She's the one who asked me to speak to you in the first place. She wanted to know if you had consented to sell us the land."

"And you told her 'yes,' thereby assuring yourself of a write-up in this morning's paper."

"No." She shook her head, sending her hair flying. Last night's headache hadn't been slept away. It was pounding, or was that her heart? "I didn't feel well. I didn't want to go into any lengthy explanations. As a delaying tactic, I told her that you hadn't exactly said 'no'." She licked her lips. "Which . . . which you haven't."

She looked at his hard expression. He wasn't buying it. "I swear, Logan. I had no idea she would run to the newspaper with this!"

"But you can't be all that upset over it. Look what a heroine it makes of you."

"What about you? You come off sounding like a potential general for the Salvation Army!"

"Something we both know I don't deserve."

"Damn right. Are you angry with me because now you have to give up one acre of your precious property? Which is just one of the many material things you constantly remind everyone was hard for you to come by."

"You're making me mad, Dani," he said in a voice suddenly soft and much more threatening.

"Why else would you come forcing your way into my room?"

"Because," he said silkily, "we struck a bargain that had nothing to do with Friends of Children, or that property, or anything except the two of us." He slowly began to unbutton his shirt.

"What are you doing?" she asked on a fine thread of breath.

"I'm about to cancel the debt." His shirt was unbuttoned now, the tails hanging loosely around his hips. "You got what you wanted, Dani. Now I'm committed to releasing that land whether I want to or not. It's time you lived up to your end of the bargain." He whipped his belt from its loops, unsnapped and unzipped the slacks.

"No," she whispered, backing as far as she could against the headboard. "Logan, you're not thinking clearly. You're angry. I understand. I'm sorry for what's happened."

"So am I. I didn't want it to be this way."

"You're doing this because your pride's been hurt. I walked out on you."

"I could live with that. What I can't tolerate is that you walked out and then pulled this sneaky stunt." He waved a hand down toward the newspaper. "I told you from the beginning that you couldn't manipulate me. Well, you did. But by God, you're not going to get away with it."

"You mean to force me?"

"I tried every way I knew to woo you into loving me again."

He remembered his sense of utter dejection as he watched her flee. How ridiculous he must have looked with the champagne and the rose, like some besotted sap gone a'courtin'. The recollection only hardened him further and he came around the corner of the bed.

"Don't do this, Logan." She inched toward the opposite side of the bed, but he caught the tail of her nightshirt in his fist.

"That's what I kept yelling at you that night we eloped. 'Don't let them do this to us, Dani.' But you just stood there while they stuffed me into that damn sheriff's car. You let them separate us, all the while me begging you not to."

"I was in shock."

"So was I when I read the newspaper this morning."

"That happened ten years ago. I was a child. I can't be held accountable."

"Neither can I."

By turning his fist end over end, he reeled her in.

"Yes, you can," she said with frantic fear. "You'll hate yourself for this, Logan."

"I already hate myself. For being a fool for the past ten years. For thinking you could be more than a shallow socialite who plays with people's lives. I'll no doubt regret this, but at least it'll all be over. After this, I can start forgetting you."

"And this is the last thing you want to remember? You want it to end like this? With a rape?"

"Is that what you'll call it?"

"Yes, because I won't submit. I'll fight you."

"Suit yourself."

"I'll scream."

"No, you won't. You wouldn't want the bad publicity."

"Neither will you. Think of that. Everyone in town will find out."

"I don't give a damn. I don't give a damn about anything but having you."

He lunged for her then, catching her around the waist and falling with her onto the tousled bed. His thighs straddled her hips to pin her down. Dani gasped in shock and disbelief, then bucked her body in outrage when he grabbed handfuls of her nightshirt and tore it open.

"Logan, stop this. Oh, God, this can't be happening."

He was beyond hearing, beyond reasoning. His mouth was hard as it ground against hers. A bone-crushing grip sealed her wrists together and hauled them over her head. The hand that held her jaw immobile bore no resemblance to the one that had stroked and petted her, loved her with exquisite tenderness, and aroused her with gentle playfulness.

He dug his knee between hers and forced her thighs to part. His body wedged between them with angry aggression. His hand scoured her breasts. His relentless fingers brought her nipples to aching peaks and she was disgusted by her own body's betrayal.

He released her from his savage, breath-stealing kiss and lowered his head to her breast. His tongue flayed her nipple. His body pumped against hers, frustrated because clothes still separated them. He groped to free himself.

"Logan."

So much despair and disillusionment went into his whispered name that it penetrated the wall of fury around his brain as shouts and screams couldn't have. His lips ceased their torrid kisses. It was no longer necessary for his hand to secure her wrists; her arms were slack. She was no longer fighting him. Her thighs were lying open and listless, no longer making an attempt to protect her softness from him.

His breath was labored and uneven as he raised his head and looked down into her face. Her eyes were closed, but tears trickled out from under the lashes. He glanced down the length of her body, saw her—defenseless and defeated—saw himself—bruising and brutal—and realized the grievous act he had almost committed.

Guilt and regret weighed him down like a steel mantle, and he lowered himself over her, in a different way, protecting her from himself. His hands clasped her head. His fingers tunneled through her hair as he burrowed his face in the hollow of her neck.

"Dani, Dani." The words struggled hoarsely,

painfully, from the bottom of his soul. "God, what have I done? What have I done?"

For long minutes they lay like that. The only movement came from his fingers, rubbing her scalp softly, apologetically. When his breathing was closer to normal, he lifted himself away from her and sat on the side of the bed. Looking down at her vanquished posture, he felt so much shame, he thought he would be sick. He despised himself. He reached across her to pull the torn nightshirt gently over her breasts. At his touch, she flinched, and it rent his heart in two.

He got off the bed. Propping his forearm against the wall, he pressed his head into his clenched fist. One knee was slightly bent as he leaned into the wall. His trousers had settled loosely around his hips. His shirt hung limply from one shoulder like the battle flag of an army that had suffered a humiliating defeat, leaving not one shred of honor or valor behind.

He sensed when she sat up. Finally garnering enough courage to face her, he turned his head. She was staring up at him. Her golden eyes were wide and wary, her lips swollen from his kisses. Even as he watched, another mournful tear rolled down her cheek.

"I know you must hate me, Dani. But I assure you, it's no more than I hate myself."

She didn't speak, but a reaction to his words shuddered through her. An indrawn breath shook in her throat before she became still again.

"I'm sorry. I . . ." He stared at the wall for a moment before dropping his arms and facing her. "Hell, there's nothing I can say."

"I'd rather you didn't say anything." She folded

the nightshirt over her front, securing it with hugging arms.

"Are you in pain? Did I hurt—"

"No, no," she said, shaking her head.

"I was crazy with rage, Dani. I swear to you I didn't know what I was doing. I mean, I did, but . . ." He searched the ceiling for answers. Finally he spread his hands wide. "I would never have believed I could be that violent, that I could hurt you. *You.* I cherish every inch of your body." His voice cracked. "How could I—"

"Logan, please, don't. This isn't doing either of us any good. I think it would be best if we said our good-byes and you left me alone for now."

"That's the hell of it, Dani." At the genuine contrition in his tone, she raised her head to look at him. "I can't leave you alone right now."

Seven

Instinctively, she sensed bad news. Whatever he was about to tell her, she didn't want to hear.

"I wasn't the only one who read the newspaper this morning. There was a swarm of reporters at my front door only a half hour before I came here. Apparently the wire services picked up the story and it went all over the state. They're here from several counties—one flew up from Houston, two from Dallas, one from Austin."

Her spine seemed to snap in two and she sagged. "They wanted you to confirm the story?"

"Me—and you. They wanted to interview both of us."

Her eyes closed briefly. "So everyone will find out that I've been staying with you. They'll think I sleep around to get donations." She could see years of hard work maligned, her credibility shattered by newsprint.

"Not if I can help it," Logan said.

"That's what you thought about me at first. Remember?"

He allowed her that shot. He felt he deserved it. "I told them they were mistaken, that you were not, nor had you been, my houseguest. I vaguely mentioned Spud."

"Do you think they believed you?"

His bleak expression answered for him. "But you weren't there, so they can't print that you were."

"Spud?"

"If she thought that's what you wanted her to do, she'd go to her grave swearing on a stack of Bibles that you'd been under her roof and in her sight since you arrived." He tried to coax a smile from her, but that was asking too much at the moment.

"And you thought I leaked the story," she said with disgust. "Would I bring this kind of negative publicity on myself?"

He looked properly contrite. "I wasn't thinking. Only reacting." She didn't reply. "You'd better get dressed," he suggested hesitantly.

Again she had that premonition that it wasn't over yet. "Why?"

"The only way I could hold the reporters at bay was to promise them a press conference as soon as I fetched you."

"Oh, God!" She stood and began to pace angrily. "How did this wind up being such a newsworthy item?"

"You're a celebrity in your circle, Dani."

She whirled on him. "Don't blame all this on me. You've been in the spotlight lately too. And if it weren't for you and your shabby, illicit deal, none of this would have happened."

She'd scored another point. He knew that was the truth and could offer no clever comeback. He turned and buttoned his shirt, then stuffed it into the waistband of his trousers. When his clothing had been straightened, he went to the door. Dani was sitting on the edge of the bed again, looking terribly lost and heartbroken.

"The reporters are convening in my office building downtown. You remember the building I showed you yesterday?"

"Yes."

"In half an hour."

"And if I'm not there?"

"They'll think we have something to be ashamed of."

"Don't we?" she asked waspishly, bringing her head up. Her eyes glowered at him.

"*I* do. You don't." He took a step toward her. "Dani, I'm . . . Nothing I say can make up for . . ." He cursed softly. How could he leave her looking so forlorn, and all because of him? "I won't see you alone again after the press conference, will I?"

"No. I'll be leaving immediately."

"Are you sorry you came back?" There was pain in his voice.

She tried to stem the tears that flooded her eyes as she looked at him. "How can you ask me that now?"

He gestured impatiently with his hands. "Before this morning, were you glad you had come back?"

"I always knew I'd have to see you one more time. As you said, it was unfinished between us. Now we can get on with our lives."

He sighed deeply. "Yeah, I guess so."

All defiance spent, her head drooped forward.

She remained silent. When she looked up again, he was gone.

Knowing she would be late but not caring, Dani took a long shower and shampooed her hair. Her makeup was carefully applied to hide the violet shadows of fatigue under her eyes. Then she stepped into a honey-colored silk dress that usually did wonders for her complexion. Today she had to add extra blush to achieve that peachy glow. The dress was a simply cut sheath with seven covered buttons from the waist to the V neckline. She filled up the V with an array of coral beads. She wore the same eelskin shoes she had worn the first night of the reunion. Her hair was only partially dry when she pulled it back into a smooth chignon.

She packed her bags, loaded her car, checked out of the motel, and drove through the familiar streets to the office building Logan had pointed out to her the day before. Webster Industries, Inc. was sedately printed in gold leaf over the revolving doors.

There was nothing sedate about the confusion in the lobby. Reporters and townsfolk attracted by the excitement were milling around, chattering loudly. For the time being, ordinary workday business had been suspended. The community was in the spotlight and the citizenry was going to enjoy the attention.

The instant she was recognized, Dani was thronged by reporters firing questions at her. "You and Logan Webster went to high school together, Ms. Quinn?" "Did you enjoy the reunion? The class reunion, that is." "Why do you work so hard for charity?"

"Ms. Quinn will answer your questions, as I will,

if you'll be kind enough to let us get to the platform. There are enough chairs for everyone, I believe."

Logan had shouldered his way toward her and placed a sheltering arm around her waist. She gratefully leaned into the hard, warm protection his body offered. "Are you all right?" he asked where only she could hear him. He led her into an impressive atrium where a table had been set up to face an arrangement of folding chairs.

"Yes, I'm fine. Thanks for rescuing me." She smiled up at him, but after a moment they both remembered what had happened that morning and looked away from each other.

"Did you get anything to eat?"

"No, nothing."

"Not even coffee?" She shook her head. "I'll have my secretary bring you some."

He seated her behind the table. She smiled tentatively out over the crowd of faces. She recognized the society reporters from the Dallas newspapers and smiled a greeting she hoped didn't appear as brittle and false as it felt on her face.

Logan gave her time to take several sips of the coffee that had miraculously appeared, then, using a portable sound system, he brought the chaos to some semblance of order.

"I really had very little to do with all of this," he said. Over a roar of protest, he raised his hands for silence. "Ms. Quinn, a former classmate of mine, is solely responsible for what we're celebrating this morning. She appealed to me with such earnestness for what she envisioned, outlined her plans for the summer camp in such an exciting, enticing way, that I was more than pleased to make the property available for such a sorely needed project."

Dani stared at him in awe. He should run for president. He even had *her* believing him. She had never told him why she was so dedicated to the cause. Her sketchy ideas had been verbalized in snatches as she raced through the decrepit buildings at the camp. Yet he was making her out to be a saint.

"Rather than steal any of her thunder, I'm going to let her tell you all about it." He turned toward Dani and extended the microphone.

She took it, but her eyes stayed with his, her lips slightly parted in wonder. He gave her a private nudge with a slight tilt of his head and sat down.

She fielded questions but supplied very little in the way of real information, giving them just enough to write a story. She let them think her reticence was out of secrecy. Actually, she didn't know how many children they could accommodate or what kind of curriculum they were going to offer. As to tuition and transportation and faculty, she didn't have the vaguest idea.

"Your questions are premature," she objected with a helpless laugh. "We've only just acquired the property, remember?" She had them eating out of her hand. They all laughed with her. "These things take months of careful planning and I haven't even begun."

A reporter in the back row stood and waved at her. At her acknowledgment, he asked, "Is it too gauche to ask how much Friends of Children is paying for Mr. Webster's tract of land?"

God! How much *were* they paying for Mr. Webster's tract of land? The only price she and Logan had ever discussed had been—Oh, Lord! She floundered. "I don't think—"

"I have the bill of sale," Logan said, standing. Her gaze flew to him. He was dangling an official-looking piece of paper at the reporters. "It's marked Paid in Full."

"B-but we haven't paid you anything!" She accidentally spoke directly into the microphone she was still holding close to her mouth.

"Exactly, Ms. Quinn." Logan handed her the bill of sale along with the deed to the property, already made out to Friends of Children. "And that's all I want for it."

The audience broke into spontaneous applause. There wasn't much to top that climactic ending. Dani was looking forward to making a hasty and unseen exit so she could get away and think.

Just as the crowd began to disperse, a gray-haired lady bustled up to Logan and thrust a piece of paper into his hand. "I couldn't believe it," she said, flattening both hands over her bosom. Logan hastily introduced the woman to Dani as his secretary. "I thought at first it was a joke, but then he was actually talking to me."

"Who?" Logan asked the flustered woman.

"The governor." She beamed proudly. "Read your message."

Logan unfolded the paper and read the brief message. Raising his eyes to Dani, he looked almost apologetic. "We've been invited to have dinner with Governor and Mrs. Hyatt at their ranch. Tonight," he added softly.

There was a ripple of reaction among those reporters who had heard, and those who hadn't were informed of this latest development with dispatch. The whole room was again buzzing with excitement, as though the invitation had been a royal summons. To the people of Hardwick it was tantamount to that.

"It must be a very slow news week," Logan said dryly. "How do you want me to respond, Dani?"

"I don't know," she answered breathlessly. "How far is it?"

Logan squeezed one eye shut and estimated. "A two-hour flight."

"And by car?"

"Too far. I'll have to fly us there."

"Oh." She would be with Logan. In an airplane. A small airplane. No one else, just the two of them.

The anxious indecision on her face brought an ache to his heart. Was she afraid of him? *What did you expect, you jerk? You almost raped her.* "Governor Hyatt is a friend of mine, Dani. He won't be offended if I call and say we can't make it. Prior commitments, that sort of thing."

Mrs. Meneffee would have her head on a pike if she refused an invitation from the governor. And Dani was certain her declining would be duly reported in this evening's editions of the newspapers. Everyone was watching her, waiting expectantly for her answer. She had no choice. "It was most gracious of the Hyatts to extend the invitation. Of course, I'll be delighted to go."

For one heart-piercing, pulse-stopping moment, Logan probed deeply into her eyes with the blue force of his. Then he turned and said into the microphone, "I'm sure you'll all excuse us." He executed a dazzling smile. "Thank you for coming."

Before Dani was quite sure how it had happened, Logan was hustling her out of the crowd and into an elevator. They stopped on the fourth floor. He led her to the end of the corridor and, reaching around her, swung open the door to his office complex.

"Oh, there you are," the secretary said. "I was hoping you could break away and get up here before the coffee got cold. Is this what you had in mind, Mr. Webster?"

She stepped aside. On a small table she had arranged a brunch for them. There was a fruit salad of cantaloupe, honeydew melon, luscious strawberries, and coconut. There were egg salad sandwiches on rye toast, doughnuts iced with chocolate; coffee, and orange juice.

"It was so spur-of-the-moment, but Mr. Webster said you'd probably be hungry since you hadn't had any breakfast. Those cantaloupes are fresh from the Valley, and that's Mae's egg salad. She works at the soda fountain in Wiggly's Drug. I eat it myself when she makes it."

Dani relieved the woman, who was obviously anxious to please her boss and his . . . friend. She gave her a warm smile. "It all looks wonderful. I don't know how you got it together so quickly. And, yes, I am starving."

The woman handed her a plate. "Fill it right up, dear."

An hour earlier, Dani would have sworn she could never eat anything again. But she found that she was hungry and she quickly devoured the helping on her plate.

"I'm not taking any calls," Logan said around a juicy strawberry when the telephone rang. His secretary handled the call. "If you'll excuse me, Dani, I'm going to change clothes." By the time she had met him at the press conference, he had put on a jacket and tie. She supposed he had had them in his car when he came to her motel.

"What are you wearing? Should I change?"

"If you're comfortable, stay as you are. I'm putting on a pair of jeans. I'm sure if this is an at-home affair, Charley will be wearing jeans, and I don't fancy flying a plane in a suit. Besides, they won't even notice me or what I have on with you around." He gazed at her tenderly. "You look very pretty today."

She looked away self-consciously. "Thank you."

To her surprise, he knelt in front of her and silently commanded that she meet his eyes. "Are you certain you're all right, Dani? If I hurt you . . ." He looked pained and made a self-disgusted sound. "We can call it off even now. Just say the word."

He was looking at her with such compassion and regret that she longed to lay her hand against his cheek. But she didn't. Instead, she shook her head and fashioned a smile out of trembling lips. "I promise you I'm fine, Logan."

He studied her carefully for a moment, his gaze roving over her face. Then he patted her hand and stood. "All right then. I'll be right back." In ten minutes he came out of the inner office looking more casual but certainly no less handsome in his jeans, sport shirt and sports jacket, and boots. "Do you want to drive your car out to my place? It would be safer parked there than on the street."

"Yes, that would probably be best."

"Follow me."

They made the trip to his house in record time. Driving past the house and stables, he led her to the small airplane hangar. A narrow, blacktopped landing strip cut neatly through the pasture.

"What happens if a cow is on your runway and you want to land?" she asked as he helped her out of her car.

"Do you see any cows in this pasture?"

"Stupid question?" she asked meekly.

With a hand on her shoulder, he turned her and pointed. "See that fence? That's to prevent such a catastrophe from occurring." They smiled at each other, and again it lasted until they remembered that morning. His hand fell away from her shoulder.

Dani waited in the hangar while Logan went through the preflight check of his airplane. He telephoned a flight plan to the nearest airport and soon he was buckling her in. Once they had taken off, she asked, "When did you learn to fly?"

"My second year at Tech. At least, that's when I started. I went up with a friend late one night. I'd had a few too many beers and I'm sure he had, too, but somehow, young and foolish as I was, he talked me into it. I loved it, and thought that if that joker could fly half-drunk, I could fly stone sober. The lessons were expensive, so I traded with a flight instructor. I did odd jobs for him around the airport in exchange for lessons."

"You've always been industrious. I remember you working after football practice."

He laughed shortly. "No telling how many gallons of gas I pumped at Grady's filling station. But ol' Grady gave me a discount on my oil and gas, you see, so I could take you out on weekends."

He smiled at her, then his expression grew serious. "I wanted to buy you presents, give you things, pull surprises. I envied the guys who could take their dates to the best places—not that there are that many in Hardwick—but I hated the fact that all I could ever afford to buy you was a hamburger."

"Logan—" Before she knew it, her hand was on his arm. Stunned, she looked down at it. Her fingers were curling around his forearm, confidently and without fear. When she looked back up at him, his eyes melted into hers.

"What were you going to say?"

The emotion in his voice and on his rugged features compelled her to answer. "I was going to say that I never minded where we went on a date. I was glad just to be with you."

He captured her hand and brought it to his mouth. He kissed the back of it softly and left it there as he spoke. "Do you forgive me for this morning, Dani? I can't explain it or excuse it. I just want you to know how much I regret it. I'd give ten years of my life to take back those ten minutes." His eyes locked with hers. "I wanted you. I was desperate when you left me yesterday. I saw the newspaper write-up as your way of mocking me. That made me livid. That's the only explanation I can offer."

She turned her head away from him and gazed out the window. It was a cloudless day. The land beneath them rolled by with kaleidoscopic perfection.

"I would never have mocked anything that happened between us, Logan."

"I know that now. The fault is all mine. Say you forgive me."

"I have to forgive you," she said softly. "If it happened because we want each other, then I'm as much to blame as you are." She found the courage to meet his eyes. "Over the past few days, if I had the brawn you do, I'd have tried to force you many times."

This time when he held her hand, he squeezed it and kept it in his until their destination came into sight on the horizon. He released her only to concentrate on setting the plane down.

Governor Charles Hyatt himself was waiting for them in the family station wagon. He drove them the few miles to his ranch. "Margaret and the kids are looking forward to seeing you again, Logan. And, of course, to meeting you, Ms. Quinn."

"I'm looking forward to meeting them too. Please call me Dani."

"And call him Charley," Logan said, nodding toward their host. "I've learned that's the only way to get along with him."

"How is it that you're on a first name basis with our governor?" she asked, flirtatiously cocking her head to one side.

"I asked him to serve on our energy commission," the governor answered for Logan. "Before I knew it, he was taking it over."

"That sounds like him."

"Thanks," Logan said cheerfully, deliberately taking her rib as a compliment.

"Don't be too impressed by my title, Dani," Charley said. "Before I got into politics, I was just a cowpuncher. You know what? Compared to handling the Texas legislators, herding cows is kids' play."

The rest of the family was as friendly and folksy as the governor. Dani liked Mrs. Hyatt immediately. Plump and complacent, she had few incisive opinions of her own, thought everything her husband said was witty or brilliant, and was an excellent mother and a gracious and generous hostess.

"We were blessed with three healthy boys and I'm grateful for them every day," she said to Dani. "The work you do with those children is wonderful, truly. When I read that article this morning about the camp y'all were starting, I told Charley I wanted y'all to come out here tonight for supper so I could congratulate y'all in person and offer our support. Charley Junior, get your elbows off the table, please."

"Did you have fun?" Logan asked Dani later as he headed the plane east, leaving a spectacular sunset behind them.

"Yes, I really did. It wasn't anything like what I expected."

"Which was?"

"Something much more formal, stiff, a state dinner. I enjoyed the family atmosphere, the children." He detected her wistful inflection.

"Do you ever wish you had children, Dani?"

The question seemed to unnerve her. She shifted uneasily in her seat. "Yes," she responded huskily. "Of course I've thought about it."

"The older I get, the more I think about it," Logan said introspectively. "Do you remember when we'd do nothing more on a date than park down there by the lake? Lots of those times we'd talk about being married. We'd plan our kids. Remember?"

Her eyes met his across the darkening cockpit of the aircraft, then turned away. Surrounding them was a deep indigo twilight, as soft and warm and encapsulating as those summer nights so long ago. "Of course I remember."

"We used to wonder how many we would have, what we'd name them. Remember all that?" Unable to speak for the swelling knot in her throat, she nodded. "If we'd stayed married these last ten years, what kind of kids would we have now? How old would they be? What would they look like? We decided they were sure to be blonds, didn't we?"

"Logan, please," she whispered faintly. She sniffed back a sob she didn't want him to hear. In a desperate attempt to lighten the mood, she said, "I'm not sure you were interested so much in *having* children as you were in *making* them."

"I plead guilty," he said with a roguish smile. It soon faded into an expression of intense longing. "I'm still interested in it."

They lapsed into a companionable silence. The lulling hum of the airplane's motor soon had Dani nodding. Because she'd had hardly any sleep the night before, she fell into such a deep sleep that even the landing didn't awaken her.

When she did open her eyes, Logan was lightly shaking her shoulder. "We're home, Dani," he whispered.

"Already?"

"Yeah, after only two hours," he teased.

"I'm sorry," she said self-consciously, pulling herself upright from her slumped position in the seat. "I didn't mean to—"

"It's okay. Watch your step." He helped her down, then went about securing his airplane.

"Logan?" She was standing stiffly against the hangar wall.

"Hmmm?"

"Is there . . . uh . . . a rest room close?"

His grin shone brightly in the moonlight as he took her hand and led her toward their cars. "Nearest one is in the stable. Can you wait till then?"

She scampered behind the wheel of her car, started it, and was halfway down the road before he had even turned around. He was waiting for her as she came out of the small lavatory in the stable.

"Better?"

"Much," she sighed, then whipped her head around. "What was that?"

"What?"

"I thought I heard a noise." She gestured toward the stalls.

"I'd better go check then."

He lifted down a battery-operated lantern from a hook on the wall and switched it on. Walking down the central aisle of the barn, he swung the light into each stall. Dani followed close on his heels.

"You'll get those fancy Neiman-Marcus shoes messed up."

"I don't care. If anything spooky is going on, I don't want to be left alone."

He chuckled and continued his inspection of the stalls as they passed them. "All safe and sound. The ponies are asleep." He turned to face her. She was so close, he bumped into her. To keep her from falling, he caught her upper arms. Her muscles tensed beneath his hands.

"Dani," he asked remorsefully, "are you still afraid of me?"

She heard the despair tearing through his throat and hastened to relieve it. "No, Logan, no. Don't think that. I'm not."

He moved her against the wall so that the moonlight pouring through the window would light her face and he could assure himself. "When I touch you, you flinch? Why, Dani?"

"I'm not flinching." She was entranced by the moon's silver sheen on his hair. Her fingers couldn't resist reaching for it. "Your touch has always made me tremble."

Eight

His hands glided up and down her arms. He dared not let himself hope, but his body was racing ahead heedlessly, avoiding his warnings not to read anything into her words.

"What do you mean, Dani?"

"That for almost as long as I can remember, your body, even the thought of it, has brought a response from mine."

"Dani." He grimaced with a spasm of relief so intense it resembled pain.

They were standing close, but her folded arms, lodged against his chest, put necessary space between them. "You could never have finished what you started this morning," she said quietly. Her gaze drifted up to his. His eyes were shining darkly in the moonlight. "There's too much inside you that's good and fine for you ever to hurt anyone, especially someone you once cared about."

"Perhaps you're giving me more credit than I deserve."

She shook her head. "No. You were justifiably outraged. You were seeking an outlet for that rage. It was natural that you directed it toward me. But you would never have hurt me, Logan. I know you wouldn't."

"Thank you for your confidence in my character. But you're wrong about the other."

"What other?"

"That you're someone I 'once cared about.' I care for you now, Dani. And it has nothing to do with us ten years ago. If I hadn't met you until three nights ago, I would have known then that you're the only woman I could ever love."

He caught her hands between his and held them close to his chest. "Why did you leave yesterday, Dani?"

Her head fell forward to rest on their linked fists. "I didn't want making love to be the culmination of a game for us. I wanted it to be more."

He let her hands go and laid a warm palm against her cheek, raising her head. "It *was* more than that. I confess that I was bitter when I first saw you. Maybe I did want to give back a little of the hurt and humiliation I felt that night we eloped. But I got over that the instant I took you in my arms to dance with you. Despite your sophisticated lifestyle, your social standing, you're still my sweet Dani. Beautiful, intelligent, charming, sexy without trying to be. I tried every way I could to let you know how I feel without coming right out and saying it. Don't you know by now why I wanted you in my bed?"

She cupped his face with her hands and leaned

toward him. His arms went around her. "I think I do, but come right out and say it anyway, so I'll be sure."

"So you'll be sure," he whispered, "I love you, Danielle Elizabeth Quinn."

She sighed his name and her arms slid around his neck. His embrace tightened as he buried his face in her neck.

"You've been such a part of me, like a splinter I've carried under my skin for all these years. I can't remember a time when I didn't love you," he said.

He rubbed her back, moving his hands over the smoothness beneath the silk, detailing each vertebra with the tips of his fingers. His hands glided past the curve of her waist to the flare of her hips. But he moved slowly, gently. He would never risk frightening her again.

"Nor I, Logan. I've loved you from the moment I walked into Miss Pritikin's history class as a new student and you offered me your desk in the front row."

He lifted his head and peered down into her face. "Ever since then?"

"Yes. You took my breath away."

He read nothing on her face but the sublime happiness that was welling inside him. His heart felt ready to burst, and if her glowing eyes and radiant smile were any indication, Dani was experiencing the same sense of freedom and elation.

His mouth lowered gently to hers. He didn't press her lips to open. His tongue remained dormant. He merely brushed her mouth with his, back and forth, breathing mistily.

After several moments she raised her head. Her

fingers plowed through his hair. "Have you gone shy on me?"

"I didn't want to alarm you."

She adored the silky crispness of his hair and ran her fingers through it salaciously. "I give you my permission."

"To what?" he asked thickly. He felt thick all over. His fingers, his tongue, his groin. God! He must be a beast. He had won her forgiveness for nearly raping her and had sworn never to hurt her again. Yet all he could think about was the sweet release her body promised for a torment that had been building inside him for ten years. "What do you give me permission to do?"

"To alarm me. Like this." She breathed through his lips. Obediently they opened and her tongue daintily explored the soft wet lining. Then, gaining confidence, it slid into his mouth and nestled there.

His hands opened wide over her back and he urged her against him. But that wasn't enough. He kissed her ravenously. His tongue plundered the sweet recess of her mouth. He enjoyed it as one would the juicy, succulent, nectar-filled center of the tastiest fruit.

Allowing them to catch their breath, he sought the underside of her jaw with his lips. Her head fell back to accommodate him. "I want you, Dani. Naked. Taking me into yourself, making me a part of you."

"Yes, Logan. Yes." She moved against him, cuddling his straining hardness with her belly.

"God, you're killing me. I don't know how I'll make it to the house," he groaned.

"Let's stay here."

She had succeeded in yanking him from a sexual fog so dense, he didn't think it would be possible ever to see clearly again. He stared down at her in total bewilderment. "Here? In the hay?"

She laughed musically. "Yes. It's right. I know it. Can we, please?"

"Baby, right now I'm game for anything. Believe me, you have me at my most vulnerable. I'm only thinking of you. Are you sure?"

She disengaged herself from his arms and turned her back. As he watched, thoroughly enchanted, she unclasped the beads around her neck and laid them on the narrow windowsill. The rest of her jewelry followed.

Then she began to release her hair. It tumbled down her back in thick luxury and he had an almost irresistible impulse to bury his hands in it. But this was her scene and she was playing it just as she wanted. There would be time for him to investigate every precious strand of hair later.

She kicked off her shoes and glanced up at him briefly through a forest of lashes before she raised the hem of her skirt and unclipped her stockings from their garters.

Logan Webster, Heartbreaker of Hardwick, lost his cool. He knew his tongue must be hanging down to the middle of his chest. His feet and hands seemed to have grown enormous—not to mention another part of him whose growth was definitely not imagined. His heart was pounding. His eyes were blinking with the frequency of a flashing traffic light. His whole body was on fire. He was being seduced by the woman who had filled his nights with fantasy. He was being seduced, and he loved it!

"Is there a blanket somewhere?" Dani asked softly.

He nodded and forced himself to move into the tack room, where he located a large old quilt. He spread it out in one of the empty fresh stalls where the moonlight afforded them illumination.

Regaining some of his senses, he extended his hand to her. Beguilingly, she moved toward him. He drew her into his arms and kissed her with unhurried thoroughness, treating himself to the feel of her hair in his hands.

"Would you like me to undress?" she asked.

"I'd like to undress you."

She smiled. "I was hoping you'd say that."

They stood in the middle of the quilt facing each other. Cradling her face between his hands, he kissed her mouth softly, with the slightest pressure of his lips on hers. Then her neck was awarded small nibbles that left a damp trail of ecstasy along her throat and collarbone.

"You smell so good. Taste . . ." His mouth melded into the modest cleavage in the V of her dress. He straightened, looked deeply into her eyes, then began to undo the seven buttons of her bodice.

They fell away under his dexterous fingers until all were released and the sides of her dress loosely covered her. His gaze left the last button and charted its way up to her face.

"Why do I have the sudden urge to be in the backseat of a sixty-two Chevy?"

She laughed with him. "I'm more nervous now than I ever was in the back seat of your car."

"So am I," he admitted.

"Why, do you suppose?"

"Because it means more now. I want it to be perfect for both of us."

"It will be."

He slipped his hands into the bodice and, moving them across her chest and shoulders and down her arms, peeled the garment from her body. She pulled her arms from the sleeves and waited for him to settle his hands on her hips and ease the dress down. Gracefully, placing one hand on his shoulder, she stepped out of it. The expensive designer dress was negligently tossed on the sweet-smelling hay.

His breath hissed through his teeth. "You're gorgeous, Danielle Elizabeth."

He didn't know what the garment was called; he only knew he liked it and that every woman in America should own one. It served as bra, panties, and garter belt all in one. It had to have been made of silk for it hugged her body like a second skin. A warm, pliant second skin. The champagne color blended with her own complexion until, in the faint silvery light, he could hardly tell where one left off and the other began.

He molded a hand to her waist. Yes, definitely silk. Her breast was a full, lush heaviness that filled his palm when he allowed himself to cup it. He moved his thumb and felt her responsive reaction through the sensuous fabric. He could see the result of his caress budding against the material. But he didn't want to exploit it now.

He slid his hand down to the gentle swell of her hip and then to the lace that bordered her thighs. It tapered to a fetching V. He forced his eyes from that hypnotizing delta to take in the long slenderness of her thighs. The lacy garters dangled vampishly on the smooth expanse.

Taking one between his fingers, he stretched the elastic toward him its entire length and looked at her with boyish mischief. "If you do, you'll regret it," she warned.

"What will you do to punish me?"

Her eyes narrowed to sultry slits. "Strip off all your clothes."

The garter was immediately released to pop against her thigh. She jumped and let out a squeak of protest. "All right. I warned you," she said throatily.

On the way home he had discarded his jacket, so she started with his shirt. She took as painstakingly long a time to get it off him as he had taken with her dress. But at last his chest was bare and her hands were moving over it with unmaidenly interest. "I love all this hair. It feels so good under my hands."

"Does it?" he rasped. "I'm glad you enjoy it. I'll try to grow some more."

It was taking a tremendous amount of control for him to rein in his passions and indulge this love play. One strap of her lingerie had slipped off her shoulder to lie tantalizingly around her elbow. Her breast was trying its best to spill from the fragile cup. Only the peaked tip was keeping her covered and him sane.

She went down on her knees. "This is my favorite thing," she murmured.

"What?" Her hands were smoothing the corded muscles of his stomach.

"Jeans and nothing else. That's when a man is

his sexiest to me. I love the lower torso of the male anatomy."

"You've admired many, I suppose." His breath was staggering up from his chest. She had unbuckled his belt, unsnapped his jeans, and was now in the maddeningly slow process of unzipping them.

"Sadly, more often than not, it's neglected and allowed to go to pot. Literally. But when it's hard and flat and dusted with fine hair as yours is, it's the most beautiful of God's creations."

His hands were in her hair, stirring restlessly, hopelessly searching for something to hold on to to keep him in this universe. "I have a dissenting opinion, Dani. And at least half the population would disagree with you. Still, I'm delighted you find me pleasurable to look at."

"I've looked before. Like the other night in the hot tub. That was most ungentlemanly and audacious of you."

He would have never thought it possible to laugh under these circumstances, but he did, a deep rumbling laugh that somehow matched the quiet riot going on in the rest of his body. "I was hoping to get your undivided attention."

"You did. I looked."

"But you didn't touch," he whispered.

She gazed up at him. "Not then, no."

He stood in mute distress as she worked his jeans and underwear past his hips. Then, like a shy flower which had come too close to his heat, her hand wilted over him. It was so light, so dainty, so precious a touch to imbue him with such a surging strength. Her caress was not selfish, it was loving. Then her arms went around his thighs and her palms pressed his taut buttocks.

"Logan." Her breath fanned him. She laid her cheek against his hard thigh. Then her lips. Light, fleeting, fairy-wing kisses. Three of them. As her head moved from side to side and her hair caressed his skin. "Love me, love me. Logan. Love me."

He eased her away gently, but there was nothing subdued in the way he tore off his boots and socks and kicked away the rest of his clothes. When he dropped to his knees onto the quilt, she was lying back, her arms flung over her head, her body totally accessible. Her legs were long and sleek and smooth in the moonlight. Her breasts were rising and falling in tremulous agitation that made their silk encasing flutter.

"You'll have to . . ." She gestured toward the lower part of her body.

Blood rushed to his head and caused cerebral capillaries to thunder when he realized what she meant. He sought the hidden snaps, unfastened them, concentrating with a vengeance on making his hands work right. The snaps were undone.

He eased the garment up. "God, Dani. You thought I was beautiful." The sight of her feminine realm made him dizzy. His vision actually blurred, which irritated him because he wanted to drink in every detail—the perfection of her skin, the soft allure of the tawny curling down.

Her navel was a jewel that winked at him as he pushed the garment above it. Then her breasts, twin erotic desserts that begged to be tasted, savored.

She sat up slightly so he could peel the teddy over her head. Her hair sifted back down over her shoulders. He hesitated, afraid that if he pressed her onto the quilt, thoughts of that morning would return and she would shrink from him in dread. But her hands came up to his shoulders, and, as she lay down, she drew him with her.

"Cover me, Logan. Weigh me down, anchor me here forever."

Her urgent words could have driven him a little crazy, but they didn't. Instead, they pierced through him so sweetly, he was filled with an infinite desire to protect. He wanted her to know how much she was cherished.

He did cover her, but slowly, gradually, so she wouldn't feel smothered. And he did let her body absorb his weight, but took care not to cause her discomfort. As for being there forever, he felt that they very well might be. He knew he never wanted to leave. Not when her mouth was so generously giving, flowering open for his kiss and the rapid thrusting of his tongue.

He nestled in her moist warmth. He was hard, pulsing, hot. He raised his head to see the effects of his presence. Her eyes opened drowsily, but they sparkled with golden flames. "I've never been loved before, Logan. Not really. Teach me what it's like to be loved." Lifting her head slightly, she touched the cleft in his chin with her tongue and he groaned.

He left a chain of scalding kisses down her throat and chest. As she watched, spellbound by the magic powers of his mouth, he pressed it against the tip of her breast and sucked.

With a shuddering cry she fell back. His caress went on and on, and with each flexing of his lips, she felt desire coiling in her belly like a tight spring. Her legs sawed restlessly against his hard thighs. The crinkly hairs tickled the insides of her thighs. That was only one of a million electrifying differences in their nakedness that made them yearn for fulfillment. Their exploring hands couldn't get enough of each other, couldn't record and catalogue the sensations fast enough.

Logan's mind was running wild and rampant, but his touch was gentle. His fingers slid down her abdomen through the silky cluster to discover her. She was warm velvet. She was wet silk. She was woman ready for man.

He introduced himself by slow degrees until he was buried completely. Stroking rhythmically, he acquainted himself with the farthest reaches of her, the innermost mysteries of her femininity. She was small and tight and creamy, a fantasy breathing life, milking him with her perfect body.

And those marvelous little spasms that soon rippled through her were like answers to all his prayers. He studied her face, and the brilliance of what she was experiencing shone through her skin.

This was the woman. This body, this personality, this soul. This taste and scent and feel. This was the woman created solely, exclusively, unequivocally, irrevocably, indubitably, unarguably, undeniably for him. If he searched the world, he would not find another who suited him more. Whether he spent the rest of his life with her or was eternally doomed to live without her, he knew one thing. This was his woman.

He reached as high as he could and let his life jet into her. With it went all that he was—his manhood, his heart and soul, his spirit.

"Dani, Dani," he whispered raggedly in her ear. "I love you so much, my love. My darling love."

*　　*　　*

"Did you really hear a noise, or was that a female wile to seduce me?"

She swatted at his hand. "I certainly did hear a noise! And why didn't you just turn on the lights," she asked, indicating the row of lights running the length of the stable, "instead of picking up one lantern with a weak battery?"

It was a warm night, but even if it hadn't been, the energy they had generated would have kept them warm. They lay entwined on the soft quilt, touching each other, exploring. They were lovers temporarily sated, idly playing with each other.

He rolled over to kiss her. "You always were too smart for your own good."

She folded her hand around the back of his head. "This was most definitely for my own good."

His finger lazily circled her breast, but his brow was knit into a frown. "Dani, why did you say you'd never been loved before?" He peered at her from under his brows. "What about your husband?"

"Are you prying into my private business?"

"Yes," he said bluntly. In spite of his serious question, she laughed.

"It wasn't love, Logan. I still loved you. And Phil . . . Well, he'll never love anyone as much as he loves himself. We went through the physical exercises of sex, but it was never making love, never an exchange of more than flesh."

He dropped a kiss on her temple and his lips stayed there as he murmured, "Do you ever see him?"

"Occasionally, but never alone. We'll run into each other and say 'hello' like polite strangers. The separation was bitter and final." She turned onto her side to face him. "I'd rather not talk about him. I don't want any reminders of him to sully my lying here with you. Just understand that this was the first time in my life I've ever made love."

"Me too, Dani."

"All the other women . . ."

He was shaking his head. " 'The physical exercises of sex.' "

She nuzzled her nose in his chest hair. "Well, you're certainly good at it."

"You're not bad yourself." He had found her fanny a delightful handful. "Ready to go inside? We can get in some more practice there."

"Do I have to get dressed?" She whined the question in a protesting tone.

"No way."

"Well, how do you propose I get to the house and maintain some semblance of decency?"

He stood and pulled her up after him. "Here," he said, tossing her his discarded shirt. "And I'll pull on the jeans. Especially since I now know that's your favorite thing," he drawled.

"I may have changed my mind," she said seductively. And what she did next shocked and delighted him. She kept it up until he moaned, "Hell, Dani. Do you want me to make it back to the house or not?"

They strolled through the soft night, whispering naughtily delicious things, pinching, poking, stroking, until they were virtually stumbling across the patio.

"Oh, look out for the glass," Logan warned just in time. He steered her around the mess.

Even in the darkness she could see that two bottles had been shattered, their contents spilled.

Lying in black, curled degradation were the petals and stem of a rose. "What in the world!" she exclaimed.

"I . . . uh . . . sort of had a temper tantrum," he said abashedly.

She stared up at him in dismay, her eyes wide and round. "Yesterday, when I left?"

He nodded. "I invented some new expletives that I really should have copyrighted. They're quite explicit and imaginative."

"Oh, Logan." She wrapped her arms around him and hugged him close. She kissed his chest. "I'm sorry. The wine, the rose, they were for me?"

"It wasn't just *wine*, it was vintage champagne," he said with a trace of childish petulance that she adored. She was wise enough to know he wanted to be petted, cosseted.

Raising her head, she caressed his cheek with one hand and his chest with the other. "Take me upstairs and I'll make it up to you."

The telephone rang mid-morning.

Coming out of a deep, peaceful, dreamless sleep, Logan cursed and stretched a long, brown arm across Dani to reach the phone before it could awaken her. He carried the receiver to his ear and growled into it. "This had better be a matter of life and death."

"Well, that's a fine greeting for an old friend."

"Oh, hell," he said, flopping back on the pillow. It was no use. Dani was shifting against him, asking around a wide yawn, "Who is it?"

"It's Spud."

Dani smiled into the fuzzy warmth of his under-arm.

"I take it you're not alone and are presently engaged," Spud said prissily.

"You got it."

"Dani?"

"Right you are."

"Oh!" she shrieked. "I'm so glad." Then, in a muffled voice, she passed the news on. "Dani's with him, Jerry, and I think we caught them at a bad time. Well, good for them, of course—"

"Spud!" Logan shouted into the phone. "What is the purpose of this call, please? You have ten seconds."

"To find out if something's going on."

"Something definitely is. Good-bye."

"Wait! I want to know all the lurid details. Like what the hell was all that about yesterday, and how was the governor?"

Logan entangled his legs with Dani's beneath the covers. Her thighs parted for the intrusion of one of his. Her arm looped around his chest. He crooked the telephone between his ear and shoulder to free his hands, which smoothed the hair back from her cheeks and lowered the sheet to afford him a better view. Looking at their bodies entwined was almost as good as feeling them entwined.

"You mean the press conference? How did you know about that?"

"Because I was *there.* I had taken Paulette to the dentist and saw all this commotion going on. And who was right in the thick of it? My two buddies— Logan and Dani. And then this clown from one of our many hick newspapers in east Texas comes running up to me and asks if Ms. Quinn had been my house guest. So I said 'yes.' Was that right?"

"You did a good job, Spud. Remind me to take you to lunch."

"Well, you could have had the courtesy to warn me first."

"I didn't have a chance to tell you the details. As you could see if you were there, I had my hands full."

"So tell me now."

"No."

"Why not?"

"I have my hands full."

After a slight gasp and a momentary pause, Spud said, "I won't even ask."

"Don't. Even you might get embarrassed."

Spud sighed theatrically. "Do you think you can haul your bodies out of bed by lunchtime? Can you still walk?"

"I'm not sure, but if I can't, it was worth it."

"Logan," Spud said in exasperation, "can you and Dani come to lunch or not? Jerry's barbecuing ribs, and if you fight off enough kids, you might luck out with one or two. I'm sure you're hungry," she added sarcastically.

"Are you hungry?" Logan asked Dani. She was taking love bites out of his bicep.

"Ravenous," she snarled affectionately.

"We'll be there," he said into the phone.

"Don't let us interrupt anything."

"We won't. Good-bye." He handed Dani the telephone, though they could hear Spud's squawking still coming through. Dani rolled over to replace it in its cradle.

"I think she said something about eleven-thirty,"

Logan mumbled. His mouth was buried against the soft curve of her breast.

"We'd better hurry then."

His hand slid down her stomach and into the cleft of her thighs. Her arms crossed around his neck and her eyes fluttered closed at his knowing caress.

"You make the sweetest sound when I kiss you here," he whispered.

Her eyes popped open and a blush stained her cheeks. "I do?"

"Uh-huh. Listen carefully and you'll hear it."

He inched down. "Logan," she groaned in heightening pleasure, "we don't have time."

"Sure we do." His tongue was now dallying around her navel.

"A quickie? Isn't that what you boys used to call it?"

His lips moved lower and thoughts surrendered to sensation.

Minutes later, he lifted his head from the fragrant warmth of her neck and left the snug glove of her body. He kissed her lightly, playfully, and her heavy lids opened to find his eyes dancing devilishly.

"We boys still call it a quickie."

Nine

"What is this stuff anyway?" Logan grumbled. He had been roped into feeding the youngest of Spud's offspring while she and Dani carried food from the kitchen to the patio picnic table. "The kid hates it. He's spitting it all over the place."

Spud wasn't impressed either with Logan's discontent or the baby's aversion to the strained vegetables. "It's good for him."

Logan suspiciously sniffed at the plate of goo. "Well, it looks like the stuff that used to speckle my daddy's chicken yard."

"Logan!" Dani's tone was admonishing, but her look was one of absolute adoration. She ruffled his hair as she bent down to kiss his cheek. Leaving the baby to lick his fingers, Logan swiveled on the bench, spread his knees wide, and pulled Dani between them. He burrowed his head in her stomach, making growling sounds and tickling her shamelessly.

"Spud, is the rest of the food ready?" Jerry called from the grill. "The ribs are done."

"You'd better hurry over here with them then. If Dani and Logan get any hotter, we'll have to send the children inside."

It was a hectic meal, with the children reaching and chattering and spilling. Dani and Logan sat as close as possible, often feeding each other bites of food and kissing between bites.

"I wanted you two to finally get together, but you're positively sickening," Spud observed. The baby was battering the plastic tray of his high chair with a cup. The other children had scampered off to play. Dani and Logan were oblivious to it all as they nuzzled affectionately.

"Leave them alone," Jerry told his wife.

"Yeah, leave us alone," Logan echoed. "What's the big deal? You've seen us make out before."

"We were wild and reckless kids on a double date then. And we're hardly at the Circle Drive-In. It's broad daylight. Shouldn't you be acting like responsible adults?"

"What I'm thinking right now is very adult. R rated, in fact."

Jerry chuckled. "Better tread lightly, Spud. We're privileged to have such celebrities visiting our humble abode."

Logan, sighing contentedly as he gazed into Dani's eyes, finally turned to his friend. "Celebrities? Us? Naw."

"Last evening's paper had a comprehensive report of the press conference yesterday. Didn't you see it?" Jerry asked.

Dani's face had once again enthralled Logan. "No. We didn't get around to reading the newspaper last night."

"Don't be a simp, Jerry," Spud said. "Of course they didn't read the paper."

"Well, in case you're interested," Jerry went on, undeterred by his wife's barb, "they made you out to be a dang Carnegie or somebody, giving away property like that."

"It wasn't so much," Logan mumbled with admirable humility.

"Like hell," Jerry scoffed. "The paper said that outfit Dani's associated with offered to buy it from you."

Dani's finger tracked Logan's eyebrow, smoothing it as she asked dreamily, "Yes, why did you give it to us, Logan? Was it because of what happened yesterday morning?"

"What happened yesterday morning?" Spud leaned across the table toward them, suddenly eager, her interest rekindled. She was a dyed-in-the-wool-romantic. Intrigue fascinated her.

"No, Dani," Logan whispered. "I wasn't buying your forgiveness. Please don't think that."

"Forgiveness for what?" Spud asked an equally puzzled Jerry. "What did she have to forgive him for?" Jerry shrugged.

"Then why?" Dani asked softly.

"Because you asked me for it," Logan whispered. Taking her hand, he brought it to his mouth and dropped light kisses on the backs of her fingers. "I had decided to give the land to you even before the . . . other."

"What other?" Spud wanted to know.

"Even as I was making that deal with you—"

"What deal?"

"—it was a foregone conclusion that I would give that land to you."

"Why?" Dani's eyes were glassy with tears. Her love was so encompassing it had to spill out.

"Because you wanted it. And it was in my power to give it to you. You always had to settle for cherry Cokes when other boys could buy their girls hot fudge sundaes. I had to go without lunch for a week to buy you a corsage for every dance we ever went to, and it was always carnations, never the orchids I thought you deserved. Now I had something you wanted. Don't you know how glad I was to be able to give it to you?"

"Because you love me?"

"Precisely."

They came together in a soft kiss of avowal and were only separated by the garbled sounds of weeping. They looked across the table at Spud. She was ineffectually dabbing at a flood of tears with a paper napkin. Jerry was patting her heaving shoulders.

"Spud, whatever—"

"It's just that it's so b-bea-beautiful."

They laughed while she cried herself out. Then, somewhat embarrassed by her sentimentality, she stood and began gathering up the remains of their lunch. "I'm just so happy for y'all. You should have been living together for the past ten years. Now you will be, and I for one am delighted."

The others stood to help her. Logan patted Dani's jean-clad derriere and growled in her ear, "So am I." Kissing her quickly, he hastened to help Jerry roll the grill out of the way of the ongoing softball game, while Spud gave her children a lec-

ture on the dangers of swinging baseball bats at
each other.

No one noticed Dani's shattered expression. It
was as though she had just been roused from a glorious dream by a bucket of cold water thrown in
her face.

"Are you going to tell me what's wrong?"

Logan's sensitivity to her mood surprised her.
She had tried to hide her sudden attack of despair
from everyone as they took their leave of Spud and
Jerry. Now she went through the front door he was
holding for her and dropped her purse on one of
the sofas in his living room. Going to the wide
windows, she folded her arms across her waist and
covered her elbows.

"Why do you think something's wrong?"

"Because you've been very quiet since lunch.
Because your eyes aren't sparkling anymore. And
because you haven't kissed me in exactly twenty-
two minutes and six seconds. I'm going through
withdrawal and you haven't even noticed."

She turned her head and smiled at him. "I can
remedy that."

They kissed with unleashed control. Then, wrapping his arms around her from behind and
propping his chin on the top of her head, he joined
her in looking out at the summer greenery.

"That kiss might keep me until my next fix, but I
still wish you'd tell me what's troubling you."

She leaned against his strength, loving the feel
of his solid body behind hers, loving the feel of his
hands, which knew every sensitive part of her
body, loving the low timbre of his voice, which

seemed to speak directly to them, loving the security of his arms around her and the softness of his breath in her hair.

"Maybe I'm just tired. I think my late night is catching up with me."

"I'm tired too." His hands slid down her chest. He was elated to discover that her breasts were unfettered beneath her loose cotton knit top. He grazed her ear with his searching lips. "Wanna go upstairs and take a nap?"

"It sounds lovely," she said as his fingertips enjoyed the hardening of her nipples. "Maybe later."

Logan immediately dropped his hands and turned her around to face him. "What is it, Dani?"

Bravely she raised her eyes to his. No matter how she backed into this discussion, it wasn't going to be easy. She knew it. It was a gut instinct that was wrenching tighter with each passing moment.

"Where do you see us going from here, Logan? What did you have in mind for our future together?"

He ran a hand through his hair. "Well." He laughed shortly. "I thought tomorrow we might go see my folks. They called this morning while you were in the shower. They had read the paper and wanted to see you again."

"I'd love to see them too." She turned her back. "But that wasn't exactly what I meant. I meant generally. Overall."

"Generally and overall, I plan on us getting married, or remarried, that is, as soon as possible. I plan on us living here and raising kids and making love every night and as many mornings and afternoons as we can swing, and finally getting old and living out our days together. What did you have in mind?"

There was just a trace of acerbity in his tone that confirmed Dani's intuition. It wasn't going to be easy. Not by a long shot.

"If . . . if that had happened—"

"Would you please face me while we're talking, Dani?" he interrupted.

She didn't want to. If she did, she might back down, make compromises, give in, and she couldn't. But she did honor his request, even if her gaze never quite settled on him.

"If we had been married all this time, it might have worked out that way and it would have been lovely. But it didn't happen that way, Logan. We're different people from what we were then."

"I'm not. I still love you and want you as much as I ever did. More."

"Okay then," she said tightly, "I'm different. I've learned that life doesn't always turn out the way we want it to. Things happen. Unplanned things. Fate intervenes."

"What does all that philosophy boil down to?"

"That I don't have stars in my eyes anymore."

"Meaning I still do?"

"Meaning that I can't just walk away from what I am now and suddenly become what you want me to be."

"I think I'm going to need a drink." He crossed to the wet bar, sloshed a shot of Scotch into a glass, and tossed it down. "What you're tiptoeing around is that you wouldn't be happy being my wife, living here with me."

"I would be deliriously happy, Logan," she said

earnestly. The first of many tears began to shine on her lashes.

"Then what are we fighting about? We are fighting, aren't we? I certainly feel like we're fighting."

"I don't want to fight. It's just that I have responsibilities I can't walk away from."

Logan crossed his ankles and his arms as he propped himself against the bar. "You walked away from me ten years ago. What makes it so hard for you to turn your back and walk away from other things now?"

She glared at him and tried desperately to corral a maverick temper. "Don't throw that up to me, Logan. I couldn't be married to you then, and I can't be now. For different reasons, but no less valid ones."

Mentally he counted to ten, his way of contending with his own temper. His jaw moved around some rather blue words, then his gaze drilled through the space separating them directly into her eyes.

"Again I ask, what did *you* have in mind?"

"For us to go on as we are now. To see each other when we can."

"Be friends and lovers, just not live together? Is that the gist of it?"

She didn't like his flippant tone or his snide expression, but she licked her lips quickly and said, "Something like that."

"No dice." He sliced the air with his hands, turned to pour another drink, and swallowed it down in one gulp. "I want you for my *wife*, Dani, not an occasional lover I see a few hours each week, like some hobby! If I wanted that, I'd take up golf."

"All or nothing. Is that it?"

"It always has been," he said with level calm.

"You're deliberately being bullheaded," she accused. "I could come here often. You could fly that fancy airplane of yours to Dallas and—"

"Play pattycake with all your society friends? Mingle with people like your ex-husband? No way, sweetheart. You should know me better than even to suggest such a thing, Dani. Whatever the size of my bank account now, I haven't changed. I still belong here, on this land, in this town, with people like Jerry and Spud—simple, hardworking, middle-class, backbone-of-America folks."

"This has nothing to do with *people*. Or social classes. It has to do with *me*." She splayed her hand over her chest for emphasis. "I have obligations, Logan, responsibilities."

"Do all those parties and balls and luncheons mean that much to you?"

"They may look like just parties to you, Logan. But the money that comes from them is vitally important."

"I concede that. And if it's that important to you, I'd be proud for you to do that kind of work here."

"But I'm already committed to work that's not finished."

"And that takes precedence over me? Over our love? Over our life together?"

Her gaze fell under the quelling power of his. She was shocked to see that her hands were trembling. The tears wouldn't be willed away, so she let them fall.

Had it come to this? She loved Logan with every fiber of her body, with every thought, every heartbeat. But she had made a commitment years ago.

It was also a commitment of love, only of a different kind. Did she have to choose one over the other?

Logan would never understand. He would try to change her mind, to convince her to compromise. She couldn't. She had sworn never to give it up. Then there really was no choice.

She drew a deep breath that pierced her soul and, in effect, killed any chance of a life with Logan. She couldn't think about it too much or she would never say the words. She forced herself to speak them. "My charity work has to take precedence."

He set his glass on the bar. His eyes carefully followed the progress of his hand as he lowered it. He left his hand curled around the glass for long moments and didn't release it until his fingers turned white. When he faced her, everything inside her shriveled beneath his contemptuous glare.

"We should do this in another ten years. It's been swell."

"Well, really, Dani, you might pay more attention," Mrs. Meneffee scolded, both double chins wobbling and silvery-blue curls bobbing.

Dani shifted in her chair. "I was thinking . . . What did you ask?"

"I asked how many buses were going over to Camp Webster next weekend for the open house."

"Two, I think, though many families will be driving their own cars."

"So how many people can we expect altogether?"

"About two hundred and fifty. Approximately."

The chairwoman turned to another committee

member. "Can you arrange to have enough refreshments set up for that many? Keep it simple. Cookies and punch."

Temporarily off the hook, Dani let her mind wander again. It seemed impossible that it had been almost two months since she had left Logan's house that day. How could pain linger for this long and still be so sharp, so excruciating? At any moment she expected to die of it, yet she held on. The tiring work she had pitched herself into these past weeks hadn't provided the healing power she had hoped it would.

"He is really a marvelous man, marvelous. Don't you agree, Dani?"

Mrs. Meneffee's question was like an exploding missile in Dani's brain. "What? Who?"

"Mr. Webster, of course." For the benefit of the others, she expounded. "He's thrown himself heart and soul into the project. He's personally seen to the restructuring of the buildings, doing some of the actual carpentry. When I spoke with him on the telephone, he assured me that everything would look spic-and-span by next week. Dani, have you notified all the television stations and newspapers?"

"I doubt we'll have television coverage, Mrs. Meneffee," she said reasonably, "but yes, I've sent press releases to everyone I could think of."

"Good." She adjourned the meeting perfunctorily, but caught Dani before she could escape. "I'm surprised that you've delegated so much of the work to be done on Camp Webster, Dani."

Dani had had just about all of Mrs. Meneffee's criticism she was going to take. She looked like a sweet little ol' grandmother, but had the single-mindedness of a steamroller and the tongue of a rapier. It could puncture and make you bleed before you even knew you'd been stabbed.

"I've been busy on other projects," Dani said frostily. What she didn't say, but implied, was that if the old bag didn't like it, she could take the shortest route to hell.

"Of course you have, my dear," Mrs. Meneffee said, and patted Dani's hand. "I didn't mean to imply that you'd been idle."

"Like hell," Dani said.

She stalked away before the old biddy had a chance to recover from the shock of hearing Dani Quinn utter a curse word. Her hands were shaking as she inserted the key in the ignition of her car. She drove home mechanically, angrily gnashing her teeth. The anger felt good as it churned through her. It was a solid, real emotion that she could appreciate after weeks of sterile apathy.

Mrs. Meneffee had some basis for criticism. Once she had returned with the deed to Logan's property in hand, Dani had abdicated much of the work to other volunteers. Especially when she learned that Friends of Children wanted to host an open house on the site before the weather became inclement.

Dani had deliberately stepped out of the limelight. She had heard that Logan was becoming more actively involved and she didn't want to risk running into him at a meeting, either in Dallas or at the site. She had appointed others to do the legwork.

But there was no way she could get out of going next week. The children were aware that something grand was about to happen. They were as excited as their parents. She couldn't disappoint them.

Still, how could she suffer any more of Logan's scorn? She couldn't tell him the reason she was so driven to do this work. He might think she was asking for his pity, and she had never wanted anyone's pity. Or would he even understand a commitment such as the one she had made? Her own husband, her parents, never had.

That brought to mind her mother and the visit they had had the week before.

"Dani, you look pale, darling. Are you ill?"

"I haven't been sleeping well."

"Caffeine. You should cut down on coffee and Cokes and tea. Ah, well, not just at this moment."

Her mother handed her a Wedgewood cup of tepid tea, which she despised. But whenever she came for an obligatory visit, she had to endure a cup of tea in the living room, a room so formal, it stifled her.

Mrs. Quinn sipped her tea and critically assessed her daughter over the rim of her teacup. "Ever since you came back from your trip to that wretched little town, you've not been yourself. I don't blame you. I hated the place from the day your father moved us there. I'll never forgive him for that."

"I was very happy there. I liked the small town."

"There wasn't even a private school."

"I liked the public school. They were the happiest two years I ever spent in school."

"I suppose you saw *him*."

It was one of those little comments that her mother often threw into conversations. They were specifically designed to put the other person on the defensive.

"Yes. I saw *him*," Dani said, putting down her cup and looking at her mother steadily. "And he's more handsome than ever. Dashing. Charismatic. And I still love him desperately."

"Don't speak like an idiot, Danielle," her mother snapped. "Your father and I did what was best for you."

"No, you didn't. You did what was best for you. I never stopped loving him, Mother. He's the only man I'll ever love."

"He's just as brash and uncouth as he ever was. Oh, yes, I've read about him. Now that he's got a little money, he throws it around like a fool. Disgusting. I despise such vulgar displays of wealth."

Dani glanced around the living room. It had been redecorated three times in the last four years. "I can see that you do," she said dryly, knowing that the sarcasm was lost on her mother.

"So, now that you've seen him again and still harbor these ridiculous notions of love, do I have to dread having him underfoot again? Your father will have a stroke."

"No, Mother. You both can rest easy. This time it's finally over."

"As sought after as he is these days, I don't suppose he gave you the time of day."

"As a matter of fact," Dani said, rising, "he asked me to marry him again."

"And you turned him down? Why?"

She stared down at her mother and regretted that they were so out of tune with each other, always had been and always would be. "You shouldn't have to ask that, Mother."

Mrs. Quinn sipped her tea noncommitally. "Your father and I are going over to that Camp Webster at Mrs. Meneffee's invitation. She called today." That was another little bombshell fired with the intent of causing an unpleasant aftershock.

And it did just that, Dani remembered as she drove her car into the garage beside her townhouse. The fact that her parents would be at Camp Webster on the day of the open house had been a piece of depressing news.

But then, Dani shouldn't have been surprised that they had accepted Mrs. Meneffee's invitation. They would never have passed up an opportunity to see just how brash and uncouth and *rich* Logan really was.

He saw her the moment she stepped out of the bus. Why had she made the trip in the bus? It wasn't a streamlined, luxury coach. It was an old school bus whose bright new paint job couldn't camouflage its lack of amenities.

She looked beautiful, if a bit tired and thin. Over a beige dress she had on a caramel-colored blazer. Her hair was sleeked back, which may have added to the pronounced angularity of her face. She was holding a child by the hand and leading him down the steps of the bus. The boy was retarded. When he saw the bright flags and balloons blowing, heard the music playing, saw the other children playing happily on the grass, he smiled up at Dani as though she were a goddess who had granted his most heartfelt wish. With a whispered encouragement from her, he ran off to join the others at the refreshment table.

Logan stayed behind the cover of trees so he could observe her unseen.

Dani was hailed and greeted both by the elite and the humble, the donors and the recipients. She hugged the children indiscriminately, and many of their parents embraced her. As she pointed out various aspects of the camp, they hung on her every word. It was evident they idolized her.

In the excitement one of the children accidentally spilled a cup of red punch on Dani's lovely dress and burst into tears of mortification. Dani yanked a napkin from the refreshment table and knelt down, but not to blot at the spreading stain on her dress. She wiped away the child's tears until he was smiling again.

This was the social butterfly?

In his gut Logan began to feel a premonition. It grew into a monster of certainty that gnawed at his conscience.

He had been wrong!

Another bus pulled up and parked under the trees. It had a mechanical lift that let down a wheelchair. The child in the chair was pitiable. Her legs were twisted, her body deformed. Unable to hold her head erect, she appeared continually cowed by the world in which she found herself. But when Dani went to her and crouched down, one bony, gnarled hand reached up to touch Dani's crown of golden hair. Her useless fingers pulled free several strands and wrecked the hairdo. Dani didn't seem to notice. She was engaged in conversation with the little girl.

Dani reached into her blazer pocket and took out a handkerchief. Logan watched her dab at the child's slobbering mouth. She did it spontaneously, naturally, lovingly, without hesitation. She didn't recoil from the unpleasantness of it. Indeed, she seemed not to think of it as a disagreeable task. She seemed not to consider it at all. She just did it as she continued talking and laughing with the child.

A couple looking miserably shy and uncertain stepped from the bus. Dani greeted them cordially and pointed out the buildings she thought they should see. The father guided the wheelchair away. The child was still smiling and making a valiant attempt to wave good-bye to Dani.

Dani's face was glowing, as though she had found immense joy in something so joyless, as though she had a secret wellspring of happiness. As though—

My God! his mind screamed.

His long legs couldn't cover the distance between them fast enough.

Ten

"Dani."

It shouldn't have come as a shock to hear his voice. She had known he was going to be there. But still she wasn't prepared to see him again. She never would be. However, it was unavoidable. She turned and faced him. "Hello, Logan."

He was staring down at her with an intensity that was disconcerting. His eyes were scanning, probing. He was tense, fairly bristling with some pent-up emotion that she couldn't begin to define. It wasn't anger or hostility, as she had expected. It was . . . She didn't know what it was.

Nervously her hands sought each other at her waist and damply locked together. "Thank you so much, Logan. Everything looks wonderful. You've worked miracles. The children are—"

"You have one, don't you?"

Her lungs collapsed as though she had sustained

a blow. Air rushed through her lips and it was impossible to draw it back again. It never occurred to her to lie or to answer indirectly. His bearing, his eyes, his voice demanded the absolute truth.

"Yes. I did," she said quietly. "She died."

He squeezed his eyes shut and bared his teeth in an awful grimace. The tension ebbed out of him slowly. First his neck, then his shoulders, and finally his arms relaxed. When he opened his eyes again, he said, "Tell me."

Now that he knew, she wanted to share the whole story with him. A tightly shut compartment of her heart had opened up. What a release it would be finally to confide in Logan, something she had been tempted to do so many times over the last few years. She did not discuss the reason for her dedication with anyone. She didn't dwell on it like a macabre obsession, but it was something she never wanted to forget, either.

Taking his hand, she led him to one of the open-air pavilions that would be used for camp activities. She sat at the end of a bench. He sat at the other end.

"My little girl, Mandy, was born physically handicapped and mentally retarded," she began without preamble. "Severely so, on both accounts. It's a wonder she ever survived the trauma of birth."

"I never even knew you'd had a child."

She smiled sadly. "There were few who did. I was thrilled when I got pregnant and suspended all social obligations I could get away with, and which Phil would allow me to. When Mandy was born, Phil was horrified by her, as were my parents and his. They called her"—she drew in a shuddering breath—"terrible names. Phil didn't even want to bring her home from the hospital. He wanted to put her into a home immediately, lock her away, sweep her under the carpet."

Her eyes filled with pain at the recollections. Logan saw the straining knuckles on her fragile hands. They were chalky white, but he resisted the impulse to cover them with his own. What he would most like to have done was wrap his fingers around that bastard Phil's throat.

"All of them were against me. I had to put up a fight even to bring my child home with me." She lifted her liquid eyes to his. "I loved her, Logan. She wasn't beautiful, by any means. But she was so helpless and needed love so badly. She was mine. And I loved her."

"Go on," he said gruffly.

"Things went from bad to worse. I dropped out of the society circles to care for Mandy. That infuriated Phil. Finally he handed down an ultimatum—it was either her or him." She laughed mirthlessly. "He didn't know how relieved I was to know he wanted a divorce. I couldn't stand to look at him, knowing how he felt about his own daughter."

She plucked at the hem of her skirt. The red punch had left a sticky stain. Neither of them noticed it. "Phil left me well provided for—a cash settlement and the house. My parents didn't speak to me for months after the divorce, but that didn't bother me. I had other things to worry about. Mandy wasn't doing well. By now, she was about two. She had surgery three times in one year. I won't bore you with the details—"

"I want the details," he said softly.

She stared into his eyes for long, emotion-filled moments before she continued. "I could never get hospitalization insurance for her. My parents wouldn't subsidize her medical care." Tears seeped over the lower lids of her eyes. She brushed them away. "They wanted her to die so they wouldn't have to be ashamed of her any longer. So did Phil. I sold the house, most of my jewelry, anything I could liquidate to help pay her medical bills, but . . ." Her voice trailed off and she swallowed hard. "There was nothing the doctors could do to save her. One night, in her sleep, she just stopped breathing."

They sat in heavy silence. The noisy festivities close by could have been a million miles away. Finally Dani said, "On the day of her funeral I made a commitment to God to work with special children. I promised to give others the care and love and help I wouldn't be able to give Mandy. It's a lifetime commitment, Logan. And one I didn't make lightly."

Logan got up from the bench and went to one of the cedar posts supporting the roof of the pavilion. He propped his shoulder against it and stared unseeing at the woods that stretched beyond.

"I'm sorry, Dani. So sorry for everything." He cursed beneath his breath and slammed his fist into the post. "God, when I think of the things I've said to you. The scornful way I judged everything you did. I accused you of being a shallow, spoiled—"

"You couldn't have known, Logan."

"But I should have known, shouldn't I?" he shouted, turning on his heels to face her. "How could I have been so blind about someone I love? You must hate me for the things I've said."

"Hate? Oh, Logan, no."

"Well, you should."

"Why?"

"Why? Because I'm a damned idiot that's why."

"You're no such thing," she said vehemently, coming toward him. "I love you. And I could never love a damned idiot."

"Dani." It took two lunging steps to bring him to her. He crushed her against him, and bent his head low over hers. "Why, darling, why? Why didn't you come to me? To think that you were going through that with Mandy alone. Why didn't you let me bear that heartache with you?"

Pushing away, she stared up at him speechlessly. "You . . . You mean you would have wanted to?"

"Yes, my God, yes," he said, hugging her hard. "Why didn't you let me know?"

"I wanted to," she sighed into his shirtfront. "So many times I didn't know where to turn. I needed you. I still loved you, but I didn't know how you felt about me. I left you at the mercy of the sheriff, remember? For all I knew, you hated me."

"All right, I can understand that. Although you should have known better. But you've had ample opportunity to tell me lately. That day I was pummeling you with insults about your little society parties, for instance. Why didn't you defend yourself and tell me why your commitment was so strong?"

"It's my crusade. I couldn't ask you or anyone else to enlist. I couldn't expect you to feel the way I do about it."

"I'll never feel the way you do, Dani, because I don't know the pain firsthand as you do," he said softly. "But I can appreciate it. I join your crusade gladly. I would have weeks ago, years ago, if only you'd asked me."

"I was afraid you'd try to talk me out of doing what I do."

"Never. Not under any circumstances, but especially if I'd known the source of your dedication."

"And I didn't want your pity."

"Not my pity. You have my love."

"You have mine. You know that. But you want to get married. You want to have children. Knowing about Mandy, you might not want to risk—"

He laid a finger against her lips. "Don't even think it. If you marry me, we'll have a baby, Dani. And I would love any child that you and I made, no matter what."

She could barely speak for the emotion constricting her throat. "If I didn't already love you so much, I'd love you for saying that."

"I mean it." His arms tightened around her. "Forgive me for all the terrible things I've thought and said about you."

"You're forgiven. I knew where they were coming from. Based on the facts you had, you had every right to be bitter." She laid her hands flat on his chest and gazed at him seriously. "I want you to know that when I came back, I had no intention of telling you about this. I only wanted to see you once more, to make certain that you were well and happy."

"I haven't been happy since the night we were separated."

"Nor I."

"It took a tremendous amount of courage for you to return. You must have known I wouldn't be too gracious toward you."

She shot him a wry look. "That's putting it mildly."

He laughed softly. "Even when I was acting like a heel, I was loving you so much, it hurt. The more I loved you, the worse I acted. I'm sorry."

He kissed her with tender passion. The misery that had shackled her for weeks fell away like old skin. Under the mastery of his kiss, she was reborn.

"Marry me, Dani."

"I want to, I want to," she repeated in soft whispers against his neck.

"Then do."

"Much as I love you, I'm still involved in my work."

"I'm involved in you. In every aspect of you. What made you think that your commitment to these children would be excluded from our love? I'd think less of you if you gave it up for me or anyone else."

"I'll have to go to Dallas frequently. You'll be expected to understand."

"I'll fly you there whenever you want. And think how convenient it'll be for us to check on Camp Webster." With a finger under her chin, he tilted her head up. "So do you or don't you want to marry me?"

She pressed his cheeks between her palms and drew his mouth down toward hers. "I do. I told you that ten years ago."

"This time I'm going to hold you to it."

They kissed again. The embrace warmed them

until he moaned and pushed her away. "Before this gets out of hand, we'd better get back to the others. We have obligations that need fulfilling."

"What about the obligations we owe to ourselves?"

He squeezed her waist lightly. "I definitely intend to fulfill those later."

They stepped out of the pavilion and came face-to-face with her parents. Apparently they had witnessed the embrace. They were both drawn up straight and unbending.

"Hello, Mother, Father," Dani said calmly. "I wondered if you had arrived. You remember Logan, of course."

"Mrs. Quinn, Mr. Quinn." Logan spoke respectfully but without deference.

"You can be the first to congratulate us. Logan and I are getting married. Again."

There was a moment of chilly silence before Mr. Quinn said, "You're no doubt doing this to spite us for what happened ten years ago."

"On the contrary, Father. We're doing it for the same reason we did then. We love each other."

"Does he know about your child?" her mother asked.

Dani's body went rigid with resentment. They would stoop that low, try anything to keep her and Logan apart, no longer because he was from the wrong side of the tracks, but merely to save face.

"Yes. He knows. He also knows that Mandy gave me the courage to get out of a marriage I didn't want in the first place, to get out from under your thumb, and to stand up to you now. Logan and I are getting married and there's nothing you can do about it. And you needn't bother sending the sheriff after us this time. Logan is a friend of the governor."

"Dani," he said with soft rebuke. He placed an arm around her shoulders, which had an immediate calming effect. She leaned against him trustingly. He could understand her flare of temper, but the only emotion he felt for the Quinns was pity. They knew nothing of love and joy. Everything in their lives was measured by a price tag. Thank God that was one lesson Dani hadn't learned from them.

"We'll notify you about when the wedding will be. Dani and I would like you to come. Now you'll have to excuse us. Mrs. Meneffee is waving us toward a crowd of reporters."

"I don't see what the big rush was all about," Jerry Perkins said, loosening his necktie and putting his feet up on the coffee table. He sipped from his glass of chilled champagne.

Spud was curled in a corner of the sofa, also sipping champagne. Her shoes had been tossed aside, and she sat with her feet curled under her hips. "Maybe they had to get married," she teased, looking at the couple snuggled together on the opposite sofa. When they didn't rise to her bait, she suddenly looked comically stunned. "You didn't, did you?"

Logan tore his gaze from his bride's face and addressed Spud. "No, we didn't." Then, looking down at Dani, he asked, "Did we?"

She laughed and buried her nose in the hollow of his throat, which had been bared when he'd whipped off his tie and unbuttoned the first few buttons of his shirt. "No. But I almost wish we had. I can't wait to have your baby."

He laid his lips against hers and whispered, "I'll do all I can to help."

The nuptials had been held a mere three days after the open house at Camp Webster. They had been harried days in which Dani and Logan had moved her personal things from Dallas to his house. They decided to keep her condominium as a convenience for the times they went to Dallas.

The ceremony had been held late in the afternoon. Only a few friends had been invited to the church service, though the whole town was in a frenzy with gossip about it. Afterward, everyone had been invited to the couple's house for a light supper and reception. Spud and Jerry had generously pitched in to help Logan's housekeeper with the preparations.

The bride, wearing amber silk, which matched her eyes, looked contentedly tired as she snuggled within the protection of her husband's arm. He had rid her hair of pins and now his hand was sifting through the long, shiny strands.

"Well, we've eaten your food, frozen the leftovers, drunk the champagne, disposed of the trash," Spud said. "Is there anything else we can do?"

"Yes," Logan murmured as he nibbled on the tips of Dani's fingers. "You can leave."

Spud sat upright. "How rude!"

"Come on, honey," Jerry said, setting aside his champagne glass and rolling his lanky body off the sofa. "I get the clear impression that we've just worn out our welcome." He lifted Spud off the couch. "Don't forget your shoes."

"Don't rush off on our account," Logan said sweetly.

"We're not." Jerry's smile was that of a satyr. "All this talk of weddings and babies has put me in a romantic mood."

"You're always in a romantic mood," Spud said dryly as she used his supporting arm to balance herself while she worked her feet into her shoes. "But don't get any brilliant ideas about babies. If you get me pregnant again, I'll kill you. Or worse."

"Naw, you won't," he drawled. "Who'd love you as good as I do?" He kissed her soundly and Spud giggled. They said a quick good night and left, their arms around each other.

"After all their years together, they're very happy, aren't they?" Dani said quietly as the door closed behind their friends.

"No more than I am." Logan placed a wisp of a kiss on her temple. "No one is happier than I am."

"Or than I am," she said, turning to him. "I feel so marvelous tonight, I want the whole world to be happy."

Catching handfuls of her hair, he pulled her face upward for his kiss. His tongue slipped past her lips with the evocative symbolism of lovemaking as he fastened his mouth to hers. He tilted his head to varying angles. His teeth nibbled at her lips. His tongue caroused. When at last they parted, she slumped against him breathlessly, laying her hand on his thigh and her head on his chest.

"Tired?" He moved her heavy mane of hair aside and stroked the back of her neck. His fingers seemed to know how to make the simplest caress erotic.

"Just drowsily happy."

"Too tired to move?"

"That depends on what you mean," she answered mischievously, and plucked at the golden hair on his chest.

"I mean that if you are, it won't matter in the least to me. It's been one of my lifetime ambitions to tumble you on a living room sofa."

Laughing, she raised her head high enough to look at him. "You're kidding! Why?"

"Remember all those times we made a lot of noise when I brought you home so your parents would be sure to hear? You'd go upstairs, then ten minutes later sneak back down to the living room where I was waiting for you."

"How did you ever talk me into that? I can't believe I had the nerve."

"*You* had the nerve? What about me? They didn't even want me dating you, much less making out with you on their living room sofa. If they'd caught us, I would have been shot." He stroked her cheek. "I wonder what they think about me finally and irrevocably being their son-in-law?"

"I'm ashamed to admit it, but they'll probably act very pleased. Even if they don't think so, the rest of the world considers us in the same social strata. And what the rest of the world thinks matters a great deal to my parents."

"Don't be so hard on them, Dani."

"I guess I should consider the fact that they were here today a giant step in the right direction. I just wish I knew they were genuinely happy for us, the way your parents are."

"They'll come around. I'll slay them with my charm."

"And if they never do?"

He touched her hair and said softly, "We won't worry about it." His kiss was tender and sweet. "But you've sidetracked me. We were talking about all those tussles on the living room sofa. If I had been shot, it would have been worth every minute."

"It would?"

"Hmmm." He pressed her into the deep cushions and stretched out above her, disregarding the havoc he was wreaking on their clothes. "I don't know how I kept myself from taking you."

"I wouldn't have put up much of a fight." She unbuttoned his shirt as he braced himself above her on stiff, straight arms.

"Now she tells me." With one hand he deftly unbuttoned her bodice and unhooked the front fastener of her bra. Pulling the garments aside, he savored the sight of her.

Gradually he lowered himself until their mouths fused hungrily. The kiss was tempestuous. Their lips and tongues were greedy and bold. "Ah, Dani. I love the way you taste."

His caresses aroused with tenderness. Gathering her breast in his palm, he massaged it gently. His fingertips brought the nipple to a tight little peak. He took the milky-tasting bud into his mouth and loved it with rolling strokes of his tongue.

Dani was enraptured. She moved against him, clutching at his hair, arching her hips into his. "Don't make me wait, Logan."

He groaned and his hand fumbled under her skirt and slip to caress the satiny column of her thigh. He found the top of her stocking and inched upward along the softest of skin. Her panties were so brief as to be negligible. He fingered the lace that bordered the legs, then worked past it.

"Oh, yes." She shuddered.

He knew what he was doing and he did it well. A sliding pressure. The lightest feathering. Stroking, circling, petting. Hastily he pulled the panties off and repositioned himself.

And she knew the ultimate pleasure of having his breath mist her. He kissed the satin rose on her garter belt. He kissed the soft hair. He kissed everything. His lips were loving. His tongue was nimble and curious. The miracle they wrought went on and on until she was splintered with shards of bliss.

He adjusted his clothes and covered her again. She embraced his body sweetly, folding close around him. "Dani." He sank deep into her dewy mystery. His mouth found her ear and the endearments he whispered into it were poetic and carnal. She reveled in each one of them as though they were secret messages from a god.

For long moments they lay locked together. Completely still. Time became timeless. They became one.

Then he began to move and the lethargy that had robbed her of all strength only seconds before vanished. She felt a new rush of energy and Logan was its source. When his body quickened with his release and he cried out his ecstasy, she was hurled with him into that uncharted, dark velvet oblivion where only lovers who have given their all are allowed.

Long minutes later Dani shifted beneath him. "Am I too heavy for you?" he asked.

"A little."

He lifted himself off her and sat up. Her eyes went wide. "Logan, you're still—"

"It's your fault, you shameless hussy."

A wanton only moments before, she now blushed as befitted a bride. "I'm sorry."

He laughed out loud. "I'm not. I've had a lot of fantasies." Wrapping her in a warm embrace and kissing her deeply, he positioned her over his lap. Her body swallowed all of his full hardness. She gasped at the new and wonderful sensations that assailed her.

"I take that to mean you don't mind," he said raggedly. His lips slid down her throat and chest.

"Ah, Logan . . . Logan. I don't mind at all."

Lowering his head, he lifted her breast to his mouth. His lips prepared the tip for the gentle sponging of his tongue. She whimpered as she laced his hair through her fingers and held his head fast. "You like that, my love?" he murmured against the flushing nipple.

In answer, her hips began to rock over him in slow undulation.

Their clothes lay scattered around them in heaps. Gloriously naked, they lay entwined on the sofa, so close that one's heartbeat echoed through the other's body.

"I guess any decent bridegroom would eventually take his bride upstairs to bed," Logan ventured. His voice was as lazy as the fingers that trailed up and down Dani's back.

"Any decent bridegroom I know would do that."

"Well, I've always considered myself fairly

decent," he said, disengaging them and helping her off the sofa. "Let's go."

Arms around each other's waist, they took the stairs slowly. "I can't wait to wake up in the morning," he said. "I've waited for ten years to wake up with my wife sleeping beside me." A loving kiss was planted on the top of her head.

"Does that mean our wedding night is over?"

He stopped dead in his tracks and looked down at her. "It's not? You're not tired?"

She smiled up at him with feigned coyness while her hand, gliding over his stomach and lower, belied that innocent expression. "Only if you are."

Groaning, he turned and started back downstairs. "Where are you doing?" she asked.

"To get a jar of vitamins."

"Vitamins?"

"Or another bottle of champagne, whichever I find first."

Leaning against the wall, she laughed softly. She watched him walk away, loving the sleek perfection of his back, the way the muscles flowed into the shallow valley of his spine, the neatness of his waist, the narrow tautness of his buttocks, the strength of his thighs. Loving his nakedness. Loving his swaggering cowboy walk. Loving the man inside who was wrapped in that dynamic masculine package.

Loving him, loving him, loving him . . .

THE EDITOR'S CORNER

Readers who are new to our LOVESWEPT romances have been writing to ask how they can get copies of books we published during our first year on sale. So I thought it might be helpful for me to point out that a list of our books, accompanied by an order form, can be found in the backs of many of our LOVESWEPT romances. (Once in a while there isn't enough space for the whole list—due to my Editor's Corner being too long!) If you send the form along with your check to the address indicated on the blank, our folks in Des Plaines will get your order back to you within four to six weeks. In future LOVESWEPT books, you'll be seeing all or a part of a listing that we put together. It gives just a few lines of description about each of our first fifty titles; if you've missed any of them, do be sure to order.

Speaking of being missed . . . doesn't two months seem too long to wait for another of Helen Mittermeyer's powerful love stories? Next month you'll be treated to **VORTEX,** LOVESWEPT #67, by Helen, and it's just the sort of dramatic romance you've come to expect from this talented storyteller. Heroine Reesa Hawke is beautiful, spirited . . . and troubled; Dake Masters is as magnetic and forceful and attractive as a hero can be. Reesa and Dake have been separated for seven long months, months in which Reesa remembered nothing about her life before a fisherman pulled her out of the storm-tossed waters of the Caribbean Sea. When Dake suddenly appears, bringing back the torrid memories of their life together, Reesa finds herself just as wildly attracted as in the past, but with a wealth of new and enriching insights into the values that had

(continued)

been missing in their relationship. Yet Dake is a changed person, too. How they reconcile their troubled past and their optimism for the future makes for a provocative and tender love story that you won't want to miss.

Another very talented Helen—Helen Conrad—provides a delightful romp in **UNDERCOVER AFFAIR,** LOVESWEPT #68. Helen's heroine Shelley Pride and hero Michael Harper certainly meet in a unique way: Shelley captures him ... literally ... in a citizen's arrest! But soon Michael turns the tables, hotly pursuing the woman he's discovered he can't live without. A merry chase follows and reserved Shelley is forced to unbend—even, at one point, to become a daring impostor! There's danger, too, though, because of Michael's work, and the lovers are almost parted by it. I'll bet that you're going to relish the way Michael "shadows" Shelley ... as well as all the other heartwarming episodes in **UNDERCOVER AFFAIR.**

It's always exciting for us to bring you new talent—and never more so than next month when Marianne Shock debuts as a published author with **QUEEN'S DEFENSE,** LOVESWEPT #69. Witty, warm, and just plain wonderful, this romance gets off to a marvelous start when heroine China Payne's mother—she's just a little batty—threatens to hire a "hit man" to go after her fifth husband. That gentleman happens to be hero Reeve Laughlin's father. What follows between China and Reeve is a love affair to remember ... coupled with a chess game that predicts the bold moves of a well-matched man and woman. I believe you'll be delighted to join us in giving a warm welcome to Marianne as a LOVESWEPT author!

Touching and funny by turns, **THE MIDNIGHT SPECIAL,** LOVESWEPT #70, is another grand romance by Sara Orwig. As you know from her biographical sketch, Sara is a mother. But the four monster children who look like angels and behave like devils in her November LOVESWEPT romance come purely from the author's imagination. I've met Sara's lovely family and I can assure you that her own children do not bear the slightest resemblance to her hero's, Nick Bannon's, nephews! Those boys have sent more than a dozen teachers packing . . . but they—and their uncle—have never met the likes of Maggie Linden! A determined beauty, Maggie prevails over mice in her suitcase and snakes in her bed. But her heart won't let her prevail over Nick. His pursuit is determined . . . and delicious! **THE MIDNIGHT SPECIAL** is *very* special indeed . . . another winner of a love story from Sara Orwig.

Do be sure to look in the back of this book for the excerpt from **HEARTS OF FIRE,** the latest historical from Christina Savage. I trust you'll find the teaser intriguing and that you'll be sure to ask your bookseller for the novel, coming to you from Bantam next month. Have a glorious November!

Warm wishes,

Carolyn Nichols

Carolyn Nichols
  Editor
LOVESWEPT
Bantam Books, Inc.
666 Fifth Avenue
New York, NY 10103

A special preview of

HEARTS
OF
FIRE

by Christina Savage
author of LOVE'S WILDEST FIRES

On sale November 1, 1984 wherever
Bantam paperbacks are sold

She was a Tryon and a lady, a proud, raven-tressed beauty from a great Philadelphia family divided by war—a family now driven to open conflict by notorious rebel Lucas Jericho, who challenged Cassie Tryon to love as never before. Dynamic, passionate opponents, soon they were swept away on a feverish tide . . . until family tragedy trapped Cassie between her Rebel lover and her loyalty to her Tory brother. As a patriot heiress in a Tory-occupied city, Cassie achingly surrendered her dreams of Lucas and his maddening touch. She would live dangerously, love recklessly, and command her father's mighty empire until she could reclaim the pirate prince torn from her arms by a brother's betrayal and the cruelties of war.

Turn the page for a dramatic excerpt from
HEARTS OF FIRE.

HEARTS
OF
FIRE

By Christina Savage

Cassie escaped into the tiny rear foyer and onto the porch. The garden, she saw instantly, was empty. Which was curious, she thought, descending the steps and looking around the corner of the house. She was certain Robal had said the rear garden, but there wasn't a soul in sight.

A joke? Not likely. Robal was noted for a total lack of humor. Unheeding of the shade and slight, cooling breeze, she hurried down the path of chipped rock and peered through the wrought-iron oak foliage of the rear gate. The drive, too, was empty. "Hello?" she called. "Louis?"

Silence was her only answer. Concerned, she stepped into the drive in time to hear a jangle of harness and see a horse and carriage emerge from the stable, the driver hidden in shadows. "What in heaven's name . . . ? Louis? Robal said—"

"My compliments." Lucas reined the mare to an abrupt halt in front of her. He leaned out of the carriage and offered her his hand. "C'mon up."

"But I . . . I can't," Cassie stammered, thrilled to see him and yet reluctant to obey. "I have guests. Robal said you were in the garden."

"I was, at the time. C'mon."

Common sense and social obligations would prevail if she hesitated. Before she could change her mind, she caught his hand and allowed herself to be pulled into the carriage.

"See here!" Louis shouted, running from the stable.

"Take care of my horse," Lucas called back over his shoulder. "She's had a long run. I expect her watered and fed by the time we get back. And rubbed down, too, Miss Tryon says."

Louis jerked off his cap and stared up at Cassie. "Sorry, miss," he gulped. "I didn't know . . . That is, I thought . . ."

"It's all right, Louis." Somehow, she managed to appear as if the whole episode had been planned. "Do as he says, please."

"But be careful," Lucas warned, sending the mare forward with a burst of speed that left Louis dodging a shower of gravel. "She bites."

"This is insane," Cassie said as they turned into the alley. "There must be fifty people back there who'll . . . Whatever will I tell them?"

"That you were kidnapped," Lucas said matter-of-factly.

"Oh, God, Lucas."

"Very well, then." He grinned, took her hand and tucked it in his arm. "Will rescued do?"

He was mad. But then, Cassie thought, so was she. And quite content to be so, under the circumstances.

The carriage rumbled down the alley, slowed for the turn onto Fourth Street, and left Jedediah's wake behind in the settling dust. They turned west on Walnut and drove the two and a half blocks to the entrance of South East Square. Seemingly misnamed—it lay to the southwest of the packed and bustling center of town—the park consisted of twenty carefully tended acres that served as a symbol of beauty and serenity in the midst of otherwise untrammeled growth. The land rose and fell in emerald swells whose sweep was broken by widely separated shade trees. In its center, protected by a ring of weeping willows, wild ducks and white swans glided tranquilly across a broad, deep blue pond that was adorned, at one end, with soft green lily pads and creamy white blossoms. Lucas steered the mare off the path and to a halt beneath a giant elm. "Walk?" he asked.

Cassie nodded her assent. "How did you hear . . . the news?"

Lucas jumped down and rounded the carriage. "My first mate returned from town this morning. I rode out immediately when I heard." He took Cassie's hands to help her down. "It's a hell of a thing."

"I hadn't thought of it in those terms," Cassie said with wry sarcasm, and then stopped short as her dress snagged in the bench seat's leaf spring. "Damn!" she cursed, falling against Lucas.

"Hang on. Let me see . . ." He held her with his left hand, reached around her with his right, and caught a provocative glimpse of ankle and calf. Almost suspended, she would fall if he let her go to free her skirt without damage, so he shrugged and gave a sharp jerk. The hem tore free, leaving a small piece behind. "Sorry," he said, still holding her though the need had passed.

Cassie caught up her skirt, inspected it, and let it drop. "It can be mended," she said with a sigh of resignation.

"But how about you?" Lucas asked. "Can you be mended?"

"I thought we were going to walk."

After four solid days of talk, the silence was blissful. No carriages arriving or leaving. No women chattering, no men deep in serious discussion. No questions, no solicitous comments to be acknowledged. Only the soft soughing of the wind in the trees, the occasional cry of a bird or chatter of a squirrel. Lucas walked at her side. The breeze ruffled his sunbleached, golden hair. His shirt was open to midchest, revealing a soft blanket of tight curls, starkly white against deeply tanned, bronze-colored skin. A broad black belt with a steel buckle shaped like a helmsman's wheel circled his waist. His nankeen breeches were cut tightly, almost too revealingly, and tucked into high-topped, soft black boots that were molded to his calves by a year's hard wear. More dashingly handsome than any of the dozens of other men she had seen in the past four days, he seemed not more piratical, but rather more natural and less ill at ease than he had in the scrivener's garb in which he'd arrived at Tryon Manor. "Is it that obvious, then?" she asked, almost painfully aware of his scrutiny.

"Your eyes betray you. You haven't been eating, I daresay. Haven't slept . . . and you've yet to have a good cry."

"Oh?" Cassie bridled. "And what makes a pirate—privateer, I beg your pardon—like yourself such an authority on tears?"

"I watched my mother being raped and wanted her to die and to be dead myself. I blamed myself, then and years later again when she walked into the sea. I have cared for Barnaby, and held his head in my arms so he wouldn't have to watch them hang our father, as I did." His voice was soft, as if lost somewhere in dreams or time. "I know about tears, Cassie. I'm an expert on tears. I am . . . an authority."

Cassie swallowed a knot in her throat. Her eyes burning, she fought her grief, tried desperately to push it back into the privacy of her heart. But so delicate a vessel was no match for her overwhelming sadness. "The Tryons . . . the Tryons are not given to tears," she gulped, and, as a great sob wracked her body, stopped and stood rigid and trembling.

"Come," Lucas said simply, leading her to the

willows. And there, hidden from the world by the soft green canopy of leaves, took her into his arms, dropped to his knees and to the ground, and held her like a babe.

The grass was cool, his arms around her and his body against her warm, a promise of safety. Society forbade her to be with a man like Lucas, but she no longer cared. In him was comfort; in him was safety. With him she needn't fear revealing her weakness. Slowly, the tension subsided and she relaxed and wept openly and unashamedly. She wept for her loss, for her loneliness. She wept for her fear and her uncertainty, for her father whom she had loved so deeply, and as all those who have known sorrow know so well, wept for herself.

Tears of anguish, tears of desolation. Hot and bitter tears that as they spilled, cleansed the soul of the poisons of excess grief. Lucas's hold was firm yet tender. His voice soothed her, and his arms gave her strength. One hand soothed her hair as her tears wet his chest. One emotion denied stifles all other emotions. The control over heart and head, the injunction not to feel, spreads. All is dulled until the door is opened and, so long pent up, a flood of emotion is released. Sometimes comes anger, sometimes fear, sometimes gratitude. Sometimes, too, comes a ravenous hunger for a contradiction of death and an affirmation of life, and even more a desire beyond all bounds to love and be loved. Blindly seeking him, Cassie found his lips, crushed her body to his, and breathed his name over and over again in her need to envelop his soul, to drink in his very being.

Lucas was at first taken aback, then swept along by the tide of her emotion. Pleasure overcoming surprise, he pressed her against the grass as his tongue slid along hers. His hands, roughly and then tenderly, caressed her sides, paused beneath the mounds of her breasts, moved gently to cup them for one brief, sweet second before continuing to the pale white of her throat and the string holding her bodice closed.

The kiss ended abruptly with the sound of laughter. Their eyes snapped open and their heads turned as one. "Oh, dear!" Cassie gasped, her voice lost under Lucas's heartfelt curse.

Two children, a boy and a girl of no more than ten years, stood peering between the draping branches of the willow. "Get out of here, you!" Lucas ordered.

The girl giggled.

Shoeless and dressed in homespun, the boy grabbed her hand and tugged at her. "C'mon, Beth."

Lucas jumped to his feet and feinted in their direction. "Go on. Git!" He added as the girl squealed in terror and the pair darted away.

Cassie rose shakily and smoothed her skirts.

"Damn kids," Lucas muttered. "Get underfoot when you least expect them—or want them."

"I think providence must've taken a hand," Cassie said, fiddling with her hair to hide her embarrassment. "What must you think of me?"

Lucas took her hands and kissed one and then the other. "None the worse, believe me. I think you're a remarkably brave young woman."

"Brazen, perhaps. Hardly brave." Her face and eyes felt puffy, but she counted that a small price to pay for the relief her tears had brought her. "We were going to walk, remember?" she asked, more kindly than before.

"All too well," Lucas admitted. He held out his arm for her to take, parted the screening branches so they could pass. "Mademoiselle?"

The land sloped gently toward the water's edge. As they approached, a mallard guided her half-grown brood to the safety of the far side of the pond. "I prayed you'd come, you know," Cassie said. "I was so lonely and frightened. Richard's been so distant, and Abigail and I don't get along at all. Jim is marvelous, as always, but I wanted to talk to you."

She smiled shyly up at him. "Do you think that terribly forward of me?"

"No." He turned, followed the water's edge. "I was thinking, when you were crying, how much I wished you'd been there to hold me when I cried."

Cassie squeezed his arm to her side. "I wish I had been too."

"I've learned something from this," he said softly. "If you find someone you trust . . . and love . . . enough to cry in front of, I've found the woman . . . that is, you've found the person you've been looking for, and you'd better not let her, or him, go."

Cassie stopped and turned to him. "Do you know what?" she asked, her fingers light on his cheek.

Lucas smiled. "What?"

"I think you're right. But—" she stretched up on tiptoe to kiss him fleetingly "—this is the wrong time and place, and since I don't trust myself, let's keep walking."

They rounded the end of the pond, startling a sleeping turtle into splashing flight. "You should have sent for me the moment it happened. Espey and Ullman knew where I was. An accident, wasn't it?"

Able at last to talk about her father's death with some degree of equanimity, Cassie recounted the events of the previous Saturday morning. "It's strange," she went on, "but I can't walk past his study without looking in and expecting him to be there and to tell me this has all been some macabre misunderstanding. A joke we'll laugh about as we sit around a winter fire."

It wasn't a joke. It was a calamity. The news of Jedediah's death had struck Lucas like a bombshell. Their agreement had been verbal, and it was a foregone conclusion that Richard, Jedediah's natural heir, wouldn't honor it, which meant he'd have to find a new investor before the end of the next week or face losing *The Sword of Guilford*. His one cause for hope had been an additional piece of information that could more properly be classified as a rumor. Billings, his first mate, had heard that the son had been cut off in favor of either the wife or the daughter. Grasping at this as a man overboard would have grasped a lifeline, Lucas saddled his mare and rode immediately and openly to Philadelphia.

He had been tempted to ask the moment he'd seen her, but had known that to do so would have been impolite. But as much as he loved her, as much as he sympathized with her grief and honestly tried to give her solace, the question had never been far from the tip of his tongue. An hour after his arrival, he was still burning with curiosity. "I won't be able to stay in town long," he said in an oblique approach to the all-important question. "I, ah, suppose you'll be living in town until Richard gets things sorted out?"

"Until Richard . . . ?" Cassie looked up at him quizzically and then understood. "Oh. No," she said, evidently troubled. "I'm afraid Richard won't be doing any sorting out."

Lucas's heart leaped, but he disguised his joy. "He won't? I don't understand."

"I mean Father cut Richard off. He left everything to me."

"It's true, then!" Lucas blurted without thinking. "Thank God!"

"I beg your pardon?" Cassie asked, unwilling to believe what she'd just heard. She stopped abruptly and stared up at him. "What did you just say?"

Lucas cursed mentally.

"You knew," Cassie went on accusingly.

"No," Lucas said, trying, too late, to explain. "Heard. A rumor. But it seemed like the wrong time to talk about . . ." He paused, threw up his hands. "The truth is, your father and I had an agreement, and I was afraid that if Richard had inherited everything, I'd be in danger of losing my ship."

"And just what did father promise you?" Cassie asked coldly.

There was nothing to be done but to continue and hope for the best. Haltingly at first, embarrassed by having been caught out, Lucas explained the terms of the agreement and the importance of receiving the money by the end of the next week.

"You couldn't have cared less," Cassie said sadly. "You didn't care about Father, didn't care about me—"

"That's not true," Lucas protested. "Asking a perfectly sensible question, under the circumstances, doesn't preclude caring."

"Caring for what?" Cassie snapped. "My money? So you can build your damned boat and sail around killing Englishmen? That's the reason you came rushing here so fast. The *only* reason. You were worried that your agreement with my father was buried with him."

"Cass—"

"And I played the fool, didn't I? The grieving daughter. Throw your strong arms around her. Tell her about your own tears. What was it? An expert on tears? An authority?" Her voice crackled with sarcasm and her eyes blazed with fury. "Tell me how brave I am? How bold? Well, what about how easily manipulated? What about gullible and trusting and . . . and . . ." Near tears again, she whirled and fled toward the carriage.

"Wait!" Lucas said, catching up with her and grabbing her arm. "I meant nothing of the sort and you know it. You're not being fair, damn it."

"Not being fair?" Cassie asked with exaggerated sweetness that only emphasized her anger. "Why, of course I'll be fair, Lucas. You needn't worry about that. I'll see my father's bargain through. You'll get your money, sir, and your cursed boat." She stared at his hand until he loosed her arm, then into his eyes. "And now"—the sweetness became acid strong enough to etch glass—"I should like to be taken home, if you don't mind. I trust you are gentleman enough not to refuse."

Lucas sighed. "All right, Cassie," he said, stepping out of her way. "Whatever you say."

"Exactly," Cassie hissed, and with a contemptuous toss of her head, she stalked past him.

A dozen expletives flashed through his mind, but none of them seemed appropriate. Lucas stared down at his reflection on the surface of the pond. A water- wind-rippled privateer stared back. He stooped down, picked up a stone, and threw it into his likeness, then wheeled around in disgust and started after Cassie.

A TRIUMPHANT NOVEL
BY THE AUTHOR OF
THE PROUD BREED

WILD SWAN

Celeste De Blasis

Spanning decades and sweeping from England's West Country in the years of the Napoleonic Wars to the beauty of Maryland's horse country—a golden land shadowed by slavery and soon to be ravaged by war—here is a novel richly spun of authentically detailed history and sumptuous romance, a rewarding woman's story in the grand tradition of A WOMAN OF SUBSTANCE. WILD SWAN is the story of Alexandria Thaine, youngest and unwanted child of a bitter mother and distant father—suddenly summoned home to care for her dead sister's children. Alexandria—for whom the brief joys of childhood are swiftly forgotten . . . and the bright fire of passion nearly extinguished.

Buy WILD SWAN, on sale in hardcover August 15, 1984, wherever Bantam Books are sold, or use the handy coupon below for ordering:

AN UNFORGETTABLE FAMILY SAGA

THE MOONFLOWER VINE

BY JETTA CARLETON

Beginning in the timeless era of turn-of-the-century America, this is the story of four women bound by love, blood and family secrets . . . four very different sisters attempting to come to terms with the past and themselves. As spirited and eternal as *Little Women*, *To Kill a Mockingbird* and . . . *And the Ladies of the Club*, here is a warm, moving and powerful saga you will never forget.

Buy THE MOONFLOWER VINE, on sale October 15, 1984, wherever Bantam paperbacks are sold, or use the handy coupon below for ordering:

LOVESWEPT

Love Stories you'll never forget by authors you'll always remember

LOVESWEPT

Love Stories you'll never forget by authors you'll always remember

 # LOVESWEPT

Love Stories you'll never forget by authors you'll always remember